S0-ARO-398

REX

Novels by Fred Yager
Rex

Novels by Fred Yager and Jan Yager
Untimely Death
Just Your Everyday People

REX

a novel

Fred Yager

HANNACROIX CREEK BOOKS, INC.
Stamford, Connecticut

Shepherd Junior High
Ottawa, Illinois 61350

Dedicated to Jan, Scott, and Jeffrey.

This novel is a work of fiction. The characters and events in this book are fictitious. Any similarity to real persons, places, companies, or incidents, living or dead, is entirely coincidental and not intended by the author.

Copyright © 2002 by Fred Yager
Cover design by Jan Yager

All rights reserved. No part of this book may be reproduced in any form or by any electronic or mechanical means, including information storage and retrieval systems, without permission in writing from the publisher.

Library of Congress Control Number: 2001131920

Publisher's Cataloging-in-Publication *(Provided by Quality Books, Inc.)*

Yager, Fred, 1946-
    REX : a novel / by Fred Yager. – 1st ed.
    p. cm.
    ISBN: 1-889262-81-1 (trade paperback)
    ISBN: 1-889262-88-9 (hardcover)

      1. Paleontology–Fiction. 2. Dinosaurs–Fiction.
    I. Title.
PS3575.A29R49 2001   813'.54
                              QBI01-700481

Published by:
Hannacroix Creek Books, Inc.
1127 High Ridge Road, PMB 110
Stamford, CT 06905-1203
e-mail: Hannacroix@aol.com
URL: http://www.Hannacroix.com

CHAPTER ONE

Margaret Ross missed her son Davy more than she ever imagined. He was going to be eleven years old in two weeks and neither she nor her husband would be there to help him celebrate the occasion.

Instead, Sam and Margaret Ross were stuck on the side of Mount Kilimanjaro in Africa looking for a legendary dinosaur graveyard. So far, all they'd been able to find were a few fossil imprints and hardly any fossilized dinosaur skeletons. Margaret was starting to wonder if the whole thing was a hoax, designed to make her employer, the Natural History Museum of New York, look stupid.

She also began to think that maybe they made a mistake leaving Davy back in Manhattan with his grandmother. Sam had wanted to bring him along, but Margaret felt uneasy. They had never been to this part of the world before, and they weren't sure what they might find or how they would be reeived. Not everyone liked it when strangers dug up their land, and that's precisely what Sam and Margaret did. They dug up the land wherever they went.

Sam and Margaret Ross were paleontologists, studying all things prehistoric. A good part of their job involved digging and even called their expeditions "digs."

They had been in Africa for almost a month and, so far, the dig had been a bust. Margaret tried to convince Sam to give up the search and go home. The idea that a mass dinosaur graveyard existed in the area was pure speculation anyway.

Just over one year earlier, a nearly intact skull of a *Tyrannosaurus* was discovered in the Sahara desert to the north. A few months later, scientists found more fossilized dinosaur skeletons in a line that pointed from the Sahara toward Mount Kilimanjaro. This prompted the theory that a caravan of dinosaurs searching for food and water had traveled across a large part of Africa and may have stopped at Kilimanjaro for a bite. It was Margaret's belief that 60 million years ago Mount Kilimanjaro was probably an active volcano and would not have offered much in the way of food.

Two more weeks of searching around the base of the mountain had only produced a few fossil imprints of dinosaur tracks, but no fossilized skeletons. Margaret resumed her campaign to end the expedition.

"If we left now," she said, "we might even be able to make it home for Davy's birthday."

"But we're close," said Sam. "I can feel it."

"Even if we are," Margaret persisted, "how could we possibly find anything? This is a jungle. We're near the equator. Whatever was here 50 or 60 million years ago has long since evolved into the ecosystem. No fossils, just fossil fuel."

Sam was about to respond when his attention shifted to something over Margaret's shoulder.

"What?" asked Margaret as she turned to see where her husband was staring.

As soon as she saw it, she knew they were not leaving.

Through the tall trees and across a wide gorge, about halfway up the western slope, was a valley in the clouds. Shrouded in an eerie white mist, it looked timeless, mystical, and full of wonder

"That's it!" cried Sam. "That's what we're looking for."

Margaret just shook her head.

"You know I'm right," Sam continued. "All the best paleontology discoveries occur around geological anomalies. A valley in the clouds, Margaret! It's a perfect example of a geological anomaly. We'll make it up to Davy. I promise."

Looking at the valley, Margaret felt a sense of dread. She had her own thoughts about anomalies. An anomaly was something that shouldn't be. And Margaret believed in her heart that she and her husband should not be in that valley. Something about the place disturbed her.

3

She just couldn't put her finger on it. The only word that came to mind to describe the feeling was "primeval."

As it turned out, Mount Kilimanjaro was full of geological anomalies. It was Africa's highest peak, rising to nearly four miles above sea level. Its crest was snow-covered all year round, yet it was only a short distance from the equator, traditionally the warmest spot on the planet. Because of its location and size, the mountain contained a variety of ecosystems ranging from tropical rain forest jungles to frozen ice caps.

After a half-day's hike, Sam and Margaret found a small patch of land overlooking the valley. They had the crew set up base camp with the mountain rising up on one side and a steep drop to the valley in the clouds on the other.

While Margaret assembled her equipment, Sam made preparations to go down into the valley.

"It's getting late, Sam," said Margaret. "Can't this wait until tomorrow?"

"I just want to take a quick look. I'm not even taking any digging equipment with me."

"But we only have a few hours of daylight left."

"I'll be back in two hours, tops," he said, grabbing a small backpack. He kissed her cheek and headed off.

As paleontologists go, Sam and Margaret made a good team. She was a whiz with computers and Sam loved to dig. So while he did most of the manual labor, she analyzed the results on sophisticated computers and carbon meters.

Dressed in matching khaki Hunting World outfits, they looked like members of the same army. Only instead of weapons, they carried scientific instruments and digging tools.

4

Sam was tall and lanky with the bleach blond hair of a surfer, even though he'd never attempted the sport. Margaret had the prettiest face Sam had ever seen, and a smile that always made him feel warm inside.

Since they enjoyed each other's company more than anyone else's, going off for months at a time was never much of problem. But then Davy was born and things changed. While Sam still wanted to be in the field all the time, Margaret's maternal nesting instincts took over. She would stay home with the baby while Sam went off on his own.

When Davy was six, they started bringing him along. In fact, this was the first time in nearly four years they had left him behind, and now Margaret was sorry they did. This particular region of Africa turned out to be a very friendly place and the Tanzanians welcomed them.

Davy would have loved Africa. With all the animals roaming around, it was like living in a zoo. Monkeys scurried through the trees like squirrels, gazelles ran in herds like deer while giraffes and zebras were as plentiful as horses.

Margaret finished setting up her gear and stepped out of the tent the Tanzanian crew had erected. She looked out over the mysterious valley, wondering what was hidden down there beneath the clouds.

She checked her watch. Sam had been gone for only an hour. It seemed longer. Normally, Margaret enjoyed time alone with her gadgets. But she suddenly felt lonely and a little frightened.

There was only an hour of light left before sunset and as she looked out over the valley, she saw lightning flash on the horizon. A storm was coming.

Down beneath the clouds, near the floor of the valley, Sam found himself in a tropical rain forest full of lush green plants and wildlife. This both excited and discouraged him. It excited him that such a thing could exist at this altitude but it also depressed him. He knew that if this were the location of the legendary dinosaur graveyard, any remains would have long since deteriorated in the hot humid climate.

After about an hour, all Sam found were a few bones of an animal that could be related to dinosaurs, but since these bones had not fossilzed they were probably only a few thousand years old. Deciding to check on them anyway, he collected some samples and put them in his backpack.

Sam was about to begin the climb back to camp when he tripped over a rock, landing face-first in the moldy, damp earth. He started to push himself up when he saw something next to the rock, partially concealed by a large green leaf. He pushed the leaf aside and found a brownish colored, oval-shaped object about the size of a large softball.

An egg. A fairly large egg. He quickly looked around to see if any crocodiles were lying about. Looking closer, he began to feel the hairs on the back of his neck stand up. This was no crocodile egg. He reached out and touched it. An extra layer of leathery substance covered the shell. It suddenly occurred to Sam that he had only seen eggs like this in books. A mixture of excitement and concern made him feel dizzy. This can't be possible, he thought. He reached down and gently picked up the egg. It felt warm. Something moved inside. He put the egg to his ear and listened.

A breath caught in Sam's chest. He ran his finger along the leathery exterior. There had to be a reasonable explanation. A new species, perhaps? There was one way to be sure. Let Margaret run her tests. He removed a bandana from around his neck, gently wrapped the egg in it, and then placed the egg in his backpack. Taking one more look around for the creature that had left the egg, Sam began his ascent back to base camp.

When Sam reached the camp he noticed that the Tanzanian crew had left.

Margaret was typing on her computer as he entered the tent.

"Where'd everybody go?" asked Sam.

"As soon as they finished setting up, the leader asked if they could return to their village at the foot of the mountain," said Margaret. "I got the feeling they didn't like being up here. They'll be back in the morning."

"What are you doing?"

"I'm just sending Davy an e-mail of some pictures I took of our campsite," she said. "How'd it go down below?"

"I'm not sure," said Sam. "I need you to run some tests on something."

"Let's take a look."

Sam reached into his back pack and took out the egg-shaped object.

"Humor me, okay?" said Sam. "Do a quick DNA test and then some carbon meter readings."

"An egg?" asked Margaret.

"I think so," said Sam.

Margaret took the object and carefully scraped a small sample from the strange coating.

"This could take some time," she said. "Why don't you start dinner?"

"Okay," said Sam. He grabbed some supplies and went outside while Margaret sat down behind the computer.

"Let's see what we have here," said Margaret as she punched in some codes.

The screen blinked and strings of DNA possibilities rippled across the monitor.

Margaret leaned back in her chair, figuring the test could take a while, especially if this was a new species. But then the rippling stopped and the name and image of the DNA match appeared on the screen.

"That can't be right," she said.

Outside in the clearing, Sam set a table for two. He glanced back at the tent as he took out a bottle of champagne and placed it in a bucket next to the table. He then arranged some yellow and red flowers in a china vase, which he set in the center of the table. Finally, he lit a pair of tall white candles and stood back.

If you didn't know you were in a campsite, you might think you were in a fancy restaurant somewhere.

The table ready, Sam headed back to the tent, stopping at the entrance to watch as Margaret swabbed the egg with a chemical compound that was supposed to help tell how old something was. She coated an area and then pointed a strange contraption that gave off a weird purple light. When this light hit the chemical, it gave off a bright green color. Depending on the color and the code it went with, Margaret could guess within a few million years how old something was. She saw Sam standing in the doorway.

"Something's not working here," she said. "Maybe the batteries are dying."

"You just don't want to believe it, do you?"

"Believe what?"

"This," Sam said, holding up the egg.

"What's to believe?" said Margaret as she snatched the egg out of his hands. When he tried to grab for it, she held it close to her chest.

"Take it easy. You might break it," he said.

"Break it?" said Margaret. "If this is what the DNA says it is, it has survived what, millions of years of floods, earthquakes, and God knows what. I hardly think it's in any danger from me. The carbon meter is just giving me a false reading, that's all."

She placed it down on a table next to a framed photo of Davy and walked over to the entrance of the tent. She looked outside at the setting sun.

"No, it's not," said Sam.

"What are you saying?"

"It's going to hatch any day now."

"Right," muttered Margaret sarcastically. She looked at Sam closely to see if he was holding back a smile or something. He had a stethescope, the kind doctors use, in his hand.

"Where did you get that?" asked Margaret.

"From our medical supplies. Just listen." He handed her the stethoscope.

"You're serious,":she said. "Okay."

"She put the stethescope around her neck and approached the oval-shaped object. She gently placed the metal end of the stethoscope against the egg and listened.

Smiling at first, Margaret's eyes began to widen. She backed away from the object, taking the stethoscope from around her neck, and stared at the egg.

"It must be a new species, then."

9

"You saw the DNA match," said Sam as he walked out of the tent with Margaret following behind him. She glanced back at the egg and shook her head.

"Then the DNA reading is wrong."

"It's not a new species, Margaret," continued Sam. "It just hasn't been seen in a few million years. Come on out here."

She followed Sam out of the tent, still shaking her head.

Sam reached into the champagne bucket and pulled out the bottle. He poured two glasses and handed one to Margaret.

"To the discovery of the century," said Sam, raising his glass for a toast.

"If you're right, it's more like the discovery of the millennium," said Margaret. "Berenson is going to die of envy."

Margaret touched her glass to Sam's. "The museum will name a wing after you."

"After *us*, Mrs. Ross."

Sam took Margaret in his arms and let her lean back against him as they looked out over the valley in the clouds.

Suddenly, a strong gust of wind came from out of nowhere and blew some papers off a table inside the tent. "My reports!" Sam yelled, and rushed back into the tent.

Margaret stayed outside and tried to contemplate the enormity of their discovery. She couldn't stop grinning. Every book in their field would have to be rewritten. Every reference to extinction regarding this particular species would have to be erased. What was she thinking? The world would never be the same! If her readings were verified, nothing would ever be the same again.

She wished Davy were here to share their joy.

Suddenly, she sensed a change in the weather and looked up at the sky.

Dark storm clouds that had seemed miles away before were now moving fast toward their camp. Lightning flashed across the western sky.

In the jungle, on the far side of the campsite, someone was using a machete to hack through the thick underbrush. The figure stopped when it reached the clearing. A hand reached out and moved some leaves away to reveal the campsite and the storm approaching from the distance.

Inside the tent, Sam and Margaret tried to secure their belongings. Another powerful wind gust blew through, knocking over more equipment.

As they bent over to collect their gear, an even stronger gust knocked the egg off the table and into an open music box lying next to a cot. Sam and Margaret had their backs to the table so they didn't see the egg as it became wedged down into the gear mechanisms of the music box. They also weren't looking when another blast of air pushed the top of the box shut with the egg inside.

"Where is it?" said Sam frantically as he looked down at the table where the egg had been.

"Where's what?"

"The egg! It was right here."

"It must have fallen off the table," Margaret said, looking around the floor below.

Then she hurried over to a large traveling trunk next to the table and looked inside. "Maybe it fell in here," she said, and started to rummage through the trunk. "Not here."

"It's gotta be somewhere," shouted Sam over the rain and thunder. "You keep looking while I batten down the hatches. This storm looks like a rough one."

While Sam tightened the lines holding up the tent, Margaret picked up the picture of her son and the music box and stuffed them inside the large trunk.

"Don't want anything to happen to you guys," she said, closing the top of the trunk.

After securing the lines, Sam got down on his hands and knees and began searching the floor of the tent for the missing egg.

Outside, the rain fell in torrents. The person who was hacking his way through the jungle was now moving across the clearing toward the tent. He carried something under his arm. It looked like a brick and it had a small, blinking red light on one side. He placed the brick-like object next to a rock and continued on.

Sam and Margaret were now both on the floor of the tent searching for their miracle egg. Suddenly, Margaret looked up and stopped moving. She grabbed Sam by the back of his neck and turned his head in the direction she was staring.

Lightning flashed in the distance, providing just enough illumination to show the shape of a rather large man holding a machete and standing in the doorway of the tent.

Before either could react, an explosion rocked the campsite, throwing both of them prone to the floor of the tent. At the same time, the ground beneath them began to rumble and shake.

"Earthquake!" yelled Sam.

"We have to get out of here!"

As soon as they stood and started to run toward the door, a powerful tremor sent them reeling backward. Margaret looked down just as the ground beneath her feet opened like the mouth of a smiling giant.

"Sam!"

He tried to reach out but in a second she was gone.

"Margaret! No!" Sam rushed to where she stood but before he could stop himself, he had stepped out over the edge of the newly formed crevice. The last thing he saw as he fell into the darkness was the shape of the man standing in the doorway. The man was holding Sam's backpack.

Thick clouds of dust swept across the clearing where the campsite had been set up, blocking out all visibility. The man with the machete heard muffled screams among the jarring rumbles and thunder cracks as he made his way away from the area. He was about to disappear into the jungle when he stopped and took one last look.

The campsite was almost entirely gone. So was most of the flat patch of land where the tent and tables had been set up. A sharp cliff led down to the valley in the clouds. All that remained of the expedition was sitting on the edge of the cliff. It was the large black trunk.

CHAPTER TWO

Davy Ross stood on the observation deck of the Empire State Building thinking about how small the rest of the city looked from up here. This was the last stop of Davy's sixth grade field trip; they had already visited the Statue of Liberty and Ellis Island. But the top of the Empire State Building was the highlight of the day. Davy wished he could stay up there until dark to see what it looked like at night. But the teachers were ready to leave five minutes after they got there. Maybe Davy could talk Grandma Becky into taking him back here for his birthday.

He gazed out over the Hudson River and saw a thick fog moving in like a giant cotton ball over the water. Within a few minutes, the fog had surrounded lower Manhattan. Davy thought it was really cool to be able to look down on the clouds.

It reminded him of the last picture his mother had sent him by e-mail. It showed their campsite overlooking a valley in the clouds. That's what this looked like, Davy thought as he looked down at buildings that weren't as tall as the Empire State Building disappear in the rolling fog. He couldn't wait to get home to tell Grandma all about it. He wished his Mom and Dad were home so he could tell them, too. If only he'd remembered to bring a camera along, he could've snapped off a couple of shots to e-mail his parents his own valley in the clouds.

As he watched the fog roll in, Davy remembered how angry he was when his parents told him he had to stay behind. His mother gave the lame excuse that he'd have to miss too much school. But that had never stopped them before. Besides, Davy was smarter than most of the other kids and he could catch up in no time. He knew the real reason. He overheard them talking the night before they were supposed to leave. His Mom was afraid something might happen. She was always like that when it came to him. It was embarrassing. He was almost eleven. Didn't she know he could take care of himself? How could she? She never gave him the chance to prove it. Dad was a little better. At least he let Davy try some pretty cool stuff whenever Mom wasn't around, like climbing those cliffs along the Palisades in New Jersey.

Once the fog wiped out all visibility, the teachers proclaimed the field trip officially over and escorted the group of sixth graders back to their bus for an uneventful return trip to the Upper West Side.

All the way back, Davy thought about his parents and the adventure they must be having. It just wasn't fair. He should be with them. It's not that he didn't like his grandmother. He did. It's just that she was boring.

Sam's mother, Rebecca, who actually lived in Bayside, Queens was staying with Davy in Manhattan until his parents returned. She slept in the guest bedroom.

As soon as he entered his apartment on Central Park West, Davy knew something was wrong.

His grandmother was sitting in a chair in the living room with a telephone in her lap and the saddest look he'd ever seen on her face.

"Grandma. What's the matter?"

Rebecca Ross looked up at her grandson and felt a sagging weight pushing down. How was she going to tell him? It was all just too horrible.

"We went to the top of the Empire State Building."

"Oh, Davy," she said, trying to smile while her eyes filled with tears. Before she could stop herself, she began to sob. Davy put down his book bag and went to her. He put his arms around her shoulders.

"Don't cry, Grandma. Whatever I did, I'm sorry. Really. I'll never do it again. Promise."

Rebecca pulled her grandson up onto her lap and wiped her eyes.

"Davy. There's no easy way to say this. Your parents are missing."

"Missing? You mean they got lost?"

"Something happened. An accident. An earthquake. I haven't been able to get a straight answer. Something destroyed their campsite. The Tanzanian crew traveling with them fled the area, but no one seems to know what happened to your Mom and Dad."

"Then we have to go find them," said Davy.

"They're looking everywhere. What we have to do is pray."

After five days of intensive searching, all the rescue team found was the old trunk of clothing and personal effects, some handwritten reports, and a few bones and fossils scattered about. The giant cracks and crevices created by the earthquake had sealed shut during the aftershocks. The Tanzanian crew assigned to accompany the expedition was interviewed about what they saw. Since they had left the camp over an hour before the quake hit, most of them said they didn't see anything. Once they felt the ground rumble, they ran for their lives. A few stragglers who could still see the campsite from a distance thought they saw the ground open up beneath the main tent and then everything just disappeared.

None of them could say they actually saw what had happened to either Sam or Margaret Ross. The crew chief was chastised for abandoning the Americans.

At the end of the week the Tanzanian government issued a statement of sorrow and regret, saying the Ross's were the apparent victims of a devastating earthquake.

That same day, back in New York City, the Natural History Museum held a memorial service at the Cathedral for Saint John the Divine.

Davy and his grandmother sat in the front row, facing an altar decorated with flowers and photographs, plaques and citations, testimonials and clippings, remembrances of two highly regarded professionals.

One of the photographs sitting directly in front of Davy and his grandmother showed Davy standing between his parents at a dig in Colorado the previous summer. They all wore khaki outfits. Davy even had on a Hunting World hat just like his father's.

Davy stared at the photo and replayed the trip in his mind. He also remembered exploring all those deep caves near the dig that had pictures on the walls. They were like cartoons. His father said the pictures told stories about the people who used to live there. Davy wished his father were here now so this guy standing at the pulpit could stop talking. The man was talking about his mother and father, but in a way that Davy didn't understand. Davy was sure the man didn't really know his parents. Otherwise he wouldn't be saying all the dumb things he was saying, things you could say about anybody.

Davy turned around to look at the people sitting behind them. Who were these people? He recognized some of them. They worked with his parents at the museum. But the other couple of hundred or so were complete strangers. Davy didn't even know the man talking at the pulpit, Reverend Turner.

"Sam and Margaret Ross will forever be remembered, not only for their work as paleontologists and the scientific contributions they made, but as the loving parents of David Ross," said Reverend Turner.

"They were also our friends," he continued, "who were always there when we needed them."

As the Reverend droned on, Davy took out the picture his parents had sent him of the valley in the clouds. What could have happened to them? Why was everyone talking and acting like they were dead? They're missing, that's all. They'll turn up.

He felt a nudge from his grandmother motioning for them to get up. Great, it's finally over, thought Davy. No such luck. Now he had to go stand in a line with his grandmother and the Reverend as people walked by and held out their hands and said how sorry they were.

Davy reached into his pocket and pulled out a toy action figure of a wrestler. Playing with action figures was one of his favorite pastimes since he could take them anywhere and act out matches. He reached in his other pocket and pulled out another figure. Only this wasn't a wrestler. It was a dinosaur. A *Triceratops*. Oh well, shrugged Davy, and he began playing out a wrestling match between the wrestler and the dinosaur.

Grandma Becky looked down and saw what he was doing. She grabbed the sleeve of his suit jacket and shook her head "no."

"I'll be quiet."

"This is not the time or place to be playing with toys. Now just be still."

Davy held the figures to his side and looked down. Okay. I can be still, thought Davy. Real still. Watch this. Davy stood straight as an arrow and stared straight ahead. When mourners stopped and bowed down to pay their respects, Davy just stared right through them as if they weren't even there.

"Poor boy," said one woman. "He's in a state of shock."

Davy kept up his frozen pose until nearly all the mourners had passed.

"Grandma," he said out of the corner of his mouth.

"What is it, dear?"

"When is this gonna be over?"

"Soon, Davy."

"We need to get another search party and go look for Mom and Dad."

Grandma Becky's eyes filled with tears. "Oh, Davy."

"You'd have to write a note to my home room teacher to tell her why I'm not in school."

"Oh, dear," sighed Grandma Becky. "You know, Davy, we're going to have to accept that we might never—"

But she couldn't bring herself to say the words. Another mourner had stepped in front of her and she shook the mourner's hands.

Eventually, the line of mourners ended and Grandma Becky led Davy over to a bench next to the church entrance.

As soon as they were seated she turned to her grandson and looked him in the eye.

"Davy. Your Mom and Dad are lost. Maybe lost forever."

"That's why someone has to find them."

"They've been looking, Davy. Ever since we received word."

"But they stopped looking. Isn't that what that last report said? They just gave up too soon, that's all. We have to go over there and look for them."

That was when Grandma Becky just lost it. She started crying in deep sobs.

"Davy," she said finally. "You just have to accept it."

Davy didn't like the sound of that.

"Accept what, Grandma?"

"That you may never see your Mommy and Daddy again."

Grandma Becky broke down and started crying again. Davy put his arm around her.

"Don't worry, Grandma. I'll take care of you." As he held on to his grandmother a horrible thought passed through his mind like a chilling wind. What if she's right? What if I never do see my Mom and Dad again? What's going to happen to me?

Just then a shadow fell across Davy. He looked up and saw a bearded man dressed in black and wearing a wide-brimmed black hat. Davy felt a chill and then thought that he recognized this man. He had seen him before with his parents at the museum. His name was Jediah Berenson. There was a darkness about him and a touch of glare in his eyes. Davy remembered that his parents called him The Professor because he taught at some college.

"Such a brave young man," said Berenson as he kneeled down to look Davy in the eye. Grandma Becky took out a tissue and blew her nose.

"Can I help you?" she asked.

"I'm Professor Berenson," he said, addressing Grandma Becky. He then turned back toward Davy. "I worked with your parents, son. What's that you have there?"

Davy held up his toy dinosaur.

"A *Triceratops*."

"Indeed it is. How old are you?"

"I'll be eleven next Saturday."

"Did you know your parents actually found the fossils of a *Triceratops* in Arizona? We have them at the museum."

"He knows all about it. He was with them when they discovered it."

Professor Berenson stood up and bowed his head. "I'm very sorry for your loss, Mrs. Ross."

"Thank you."

"If you ever need anything, you let me know," said Professor Berenson.

"We will. Thank you."

"You take care of your Grandma, Davy," said the Professor, who then pinched Davy's cheek.

"Ouch!" said Davy.

The Professor walked away as Davy held his cheek where he'd been pinched.

What a creep, thought Davy. He then said a silent prayer. Please God, don't let my parents be dead. That means you have to take care of them for me wherever they are. I can take care of Grandma, but you gotta take care of my folks, okay? You do that and I'll do whatever you want. I mean it.

CHAPTER THREE

A few blocks away, in a tenement apartment on West 99th Street between Amsterdam and Columbus, Gretchen Tucker tried to decide if she was going to school or the park. She was already late. Classes had started an hour ago. Besides, the cute boy who sat in front of her in science class wouldn't be there. His parents were missing or something and there was some kind of memorial service for them. It's not that Gretchen cared one way or another. He wasn't really her type. She liked older boys. Seventh and eighth graders. He was fun to tease, though, so maybe today would be a good day to skip.

Pretty in a tomboyish way, Gretchen finished getting dressed in jeans and T-shirt and took a last look in her bedroom mirror. The face of a twelve-year-old stared back at her with a 30-year-old attitude.

"You be careful out there," she said to her own reflection.

Slipping a backpack over her shoulder, Gretchen left her bedroom and entered the living room of the long, narrow railroad apartment. In the living room, clothes were strewn everywhere, covering a sorrowful collection of rundown and worn furniture. At least the clothes covered the rips and stains on the tattered sofa and chairs. After walking through the living room, she entered a messy kitchen where dishes were piled high in a dirty sink.

"Mom! Mom!" she shouted. "I need money for lunch."

She opened the door to an old refrigerator and saw an open container of yogurt, some brown lettuce and a bottle of water. Shaking her head, she closed the door and continued on to the front door of the apartment.

"Mom! I'm leaving for school. Mom?"

She looked back through apartment at the last room where the door was closed. Her mother's bedroom. She assumed her mother was up by now. She was about to go back and knock on the door when she saw the note.

It was taped to the front door of the apartment. It said:

"Gretchen, I've got to go out of town for a few days. So don't answer the door or the phone. It might be those social workers again and we don't want them to know you're home alone. There's some money in the fridge in the butter tray. I'm sorry I have to do this. Some day you'll understand. Love, Mom."

She crumbled up the piece of paper and went back to the refrigerator, opened the door and looked inside the butter container. There, she found a single twenty-dollar bill.

Gretchen grabbed the money and walked out the door.

The next day was Saturday and Davy was in his bedroom, trying to keep busy. Whenever he stopped doing something, his mind would fill with worry. Worry about his parents. Worry about what life was going to be like without a mother and father. Today he was refereeing a tag team wrestling match between Macho Man Randy Savage and Hulk Hogan on one side, and Steggy the *Stegosaurus* and Terry the *Triceratops* on the other.

Davy's bedroom looked like someone had opened a professional wrestling toy store in the Natural History Museum. The walls were covered with posters of various exhibits and dinosaur memorabilia, while the floor and tables had become permanent resting places for hundreds of toy wrestling figures and autographed pictures of famous wrestlers. They reflected Davy's two obsessions in life: dinosaurs and wrestling. Stuffed animal dinosaurs, mobile dinosaurs, and dinosaur posters intermingled with signed pictures of professional wrestlers.

His prize collection was displayed on a bookshelf next to his bed. These were detailed, plastic recreations of every dinosaur ever discovered.

He had set up his toy-wrestling ring in the window of his bedroom. Terry was just about to pin Macho Man when Davy looked out the window to see a brown delivery truck stop in front of the apartment building.

Davy was about to ignore the truck, but the driver looked just like Jake the Snake Roberts. Jake was one of Davy's favorite wrestlers because he brought a boa constrictor snake to every match and then tormented his opponents with the snake after beating them. So Davy watched the driver walk to the rear doors of the truck.

The driver unlocked the doors, swung them open and reached into the rear of the truck. When he emerged, he had his arms around a big black trunk. He pulled the trunk out of the truck and set it onto a dolly. The trunk was almost as big as the driver, and he looked pretty big. The trunk was so big the driver had to strain to push it to the front door of the apartment building.

Davy had Terry body-slam Randy and did a quick one, two, three count.

"You guys stay here," he said to his wrestlers. "We have a royal rumble coming up."

He then jumped down from the windowsill and ran to the front door as the door buzzer began buzzing.

Grandma Becky was already at the front door talking to someone when Davy ran up behind her.

"Who is it, Grandma?"

He watched as the driver of the truck handed Grandma Becky a piece of paper.

"Just sign there at the bottom, ma'am," the driver said, sniffing. He must have a cold, thought Davy.

Behind the driver, Davy could see the large trunk. It was all beat up and scratched, and covered with stickers from all the places it had been. Davy had seen most of those stickers before. His eyes widened as he realized the trunk behind the driver was his parents' travel trunk.

Wait, thought Davy. What was that trunk doing here? They found the trunk but not Mom and Dad. This can't be too good.

Grandma Becky signed the paper and the driver pushed the trunk into the living room. "Where do you want it?"

"Just leave it there for now."

The driver pulled the trunk off the dolly and left.

Davy hesitated at first, then walked over to the trunk, reached out, and touched it to make sure it was real. Only seeing it now without his parents along side it just opened a hole in Davy's heart. A pout appeared on his face and he looked like he was going to cry.

Grandma Becky let out a deep sigh and turned to Davy. "Okay, shall we see what's—"

But Davy was no longer there.

He had run back to his room and jumped down on his bed. He buried his face in his pillow and let the burning tears pour out.

"Please, God. We had a deal. Don't let this mean what I think it means. They can't be dead. They just can't."

Behind him, the door to his bedroom opened and Grandma Becky stepped in. She was holding something behind her back. She walked over to the bed and sat down on the end. Davy wiped his eyes and watched as Grandma Becky brought whatever she was carrying behind her back around front. It was a music box.

"This was your Mom's. I gave it to her when she married your Daddy. Your mother loved that music box."

Grandma Becky handed the wood carved box to Davy.

"I'm sure she'd want you to have it," she said, standing up and wiping her eyes.

"I'd better get back to the kitchen before I burn supper."

Grandma left the bedroom as Davy picked up the music box and examined the fine wood carving on the outside. Running his fingers along the intricate design, he wondered why he never liked music boxes. He guessed it was because they were "girl" things. But this was his Mom's, so he should keep it no matter what. How does it work? he wondered. He studied the box and saw a handle on the side. He tried to turn the handle but it refused to move. Must be stuck.

He turned the music box upside down and the top opened up. Maybe something is jammed in there. Davy banged the box on the floor, hoping to un-stick whatever it was. After the third bang, something rattled loose inside. He tipped the box upside down again and this time something fell out, hitting the floor with a cracking sound.

Davy looked at the object on the floor.

"An egg?"

He kneeled down and picked it up. There was a crack zigzagging down the side of the egg.

"Great. A present from my Mom and I broke it already. Maybe I can fix it with some glue."

Just then Grandma Becky stuck her head into the bedroom.

"What's all the knocking? That's a very old music box. You shouldn't be banging it."

"Sorry, Grandma. It just got stuck. It's okay now."

Grandma smiled and left as Davy knelt down and continued to examine the egg very closely. "What kind of egg is this anyway?" he wondered. He picked it up again and held it to his nose. "Oooow. What's that smell? Yuck."

Holding his nose, Davy carried the smelly egg over to the shelf and put it next to his collection of dinosaur figures. He then opened a window to air out the room.

"That's better," said Davy as he returned to the music box and turned the handle. This time music began to play. It was an old Beatles song, *The Long and Winding Road*. Davy recognized the tune because he remembered his mother playing it at night before she went to bed. Sometimes she would play it for Davy when she tucked him in. The music always soothed him, and he usually fell asleep before it ended. This time it just made him sad.

While Davy listened to his mother's music box, Professor Berenson sat in his office at the Natural History Museum talking to a man in his 40s, wearing a safari shirt, with a two-day stubble of beard on his weathered face. The man's name was Jackson and he was pacing in front of Berenson's desk. On top of the desk was Sam Ross's open backpack with papers and bone samples he took from the valley scattered next to it..

"Will you please sit down?" ordered the Professor.

Jackson took a chair in front of the desk.

"Well, you weren't there. It was bad. Real bad. I went over the place ten times. There's nothing else."

"I saw his notes!" shouted the Professor. "It has to be there. Now go back and look again."

"It's not as easy as you think."

Professor Berenson walked over to his desk and pulled out an envelope. He handed it to Jackson, who immediately checked the contents and counted the bills.

"What's this?"

"For your expenses," said the Professor.

"You're wasting your money."

"It's the museum's money."

"You're wasting the museum's money, then. I told you, there's nothing else left."

"Well, whose fault was that? Your orders were to scare them, not blow them up."

"Something went wrong," said Jackson. "The charge wasn't that strong. It must have triggered a landslide and earthquake. I don't know how, but it did. Anyway, the point is there is no campsite to check. That trunk, and what's in that backpack were all that survived. We went over that trunk and it was just personal effects."

"Humor me anyway, okay?" snapped the Professor. "Meanwhile, I'll pay another visit to the grandmother and the boy. I just had the museum deliver the trunk. Maybe you missed something."

"What exactly are we looking for?"

Professor Berenson picked up one of the bones and tossed it to Jackson. "See if you can find more of these."

"More bones? God, you've got enough bones for three museums in storage that you haven't even examined yet. Why would you want more?"

"For one thing, what we have in the museum are fossils. Not bones. These are kind of special."

"Why's that?"

Professor Berenson walked over to a table and picked up a large piece of a hipbone. "The rescue party found this in a valley near the Ross campsite. If our calculations are correct, this and the bones in that backpack are only five thousand years old."

"Only five thousand. Sounds pretty old to me."

"Not for a creature that's supposed to have been extinct for 60 million years."

CHAPTER FOUR

Davy was deep in a dream about wrestling dinosaurs when the sound of something hitting something else woke him up. The morning sun flowed in through the bedroom window as Davy sat up and looked around. What was that? he wondered. He blinked and looked around the bedroom, listening. Other than the noise of traffic on the street outside, it was pretty quiet. Then, for no particular reason, one of the dinosaur figures fell off the shelf and hit the floor with a smack!

That was the sound. Davy looked at the *Tyrannosaurus* toy on the floor. It was lying on the floor next to a *Stegosaurus*. He then looked up at the shelf. Running his eyes over the line of tiny dinosaurs, he finally came to the egg. Everything looked normal. He got out of bed and walked over to the shelf to study the egg.

It had cracked open. He looked inside. It was empty. Whatever was inside was now out.

Davy rubbed his eyes again and scratched his head. He sensed that something else had changed but he wasn't sure what it was. He began to study the rest of the six-inch tall dinosaur figures.

"Morning, Steggy. Morning, *Triceratops*. Good morning, Tyranno."

Davy stopped and blinked. He looked closer at the miniature figure of the *Tyrannosaurus rex* and then down at the floor at the *Tyrannosaurus* that had fallen off the shelf. He looked back at the one still on the shelf and was about to reach out and touch it when the tiny figure moved its head and swiped its arm at Davy, gesturing for him to stay away.

"Agghhhh!" he screamed. Davy yanked his hand away in a flash and stared wide-eyed at the tiny creature.

"I must be dreaming," he said.

The *Tyrannosaurus* looked at Davy and then at the other figures. It walked across the shelf in search of something.

"This is impossible. You can't be real."

Davy began to follow the tiny dinosaur.

"Hey! Where are you going?"

The creature stopped and looked around the shelf at the figurines again and then cried out a tiny "squeak!"

"What is it? What do you want?"

The animal let out another squeal.

"Are you hungry?"

Davy went back to his bed and got a cup. There was a small amount of milk left in it. He tipped the cup and let some drops fall onto the shelf. The miniature creature moved toward the milk as fast as its little feet would take it and began to lap it up.

"This is incredible!".

Davy watched with delight in his eyes. He then ran out of his room and into the guest bedroom where his grandmother was still asleep.

"Grandma!"

Grandma Becky opened her eyes and looked at the clock, which read 6:30.

"Oh, Davy. Let Grandma sleep some more."

"Wake up. You gotta see it."

"Oh, what is it?" Grandma Becky said as she sat up and yawned.

"A baby *Tyrannosaurus rex* drank my milk."

"The nerve of some animals," she said, lying back down.

"No. I'm not kidding! You have to come see this."

"I'm really tired, Davy. Can't I see him later?" she pleaded as she pulled the blanket back up around her.

"Later?"

"It's Sunday morning. He's not going anywhere, is he?"

Just then Davy looked out the bedroom door and saw the small creature scurry across the hallway floor.

"Actually, he is."

"What?" she asked, half asleep already.

"He's leaving! Hey, wait!" shouted Davy as he ran out of the bedroom.

Grandma Becky re-opened one eye, shook her head, and went back to sleep.

Davy ran down the hallway and into the living room. He got down on his hands and knees and began looking under the sofa, the recliner, and the love seat. "Where'd you go?"

Suddenly, he heard a scratching sound behind a bookcase. Davy got up and went over to take a look. The sound was definitely coming from there. He tried to pull the bookcase away from the wall, but it was too heavy, so he started removing books until he had a pile of them next to the case.

At least it was now light enough for Davy to move it a few inches away from the wall. He got back down on the floor and looked behind the case. A little head stared back up at him with frightened eyes.

"Come on out here. I won't hurt you."

But the tiny animal, shivering with fear, refused to come out. Davy thought for a second and then stood up, went into the kitchen and opened the refrigerator door. What he wanted was on the top shelf in the back and just out of reach. Davy got a chair and dragged it over in front of the refrigerator, climbed up, and found himself face-to-face with a gallon container of milk. It looked pretty heavy and Davy knew from experience that this was probably a job for Grandma. But she was asleep. He took a deep breath and reached into the refrigerator. Holding the milk container with both hands, he pulled it forward. Not only was it heavy, but condensation on the outside of the plastic container made it slippery, too.

Oh well, thought Davy. Here goes. Holding the container as tightly as he could, he pulled it off the shelf and held it to his chest. Ah-hah, he said to himself. So far, so good. But then he looked down. He was still standing on the chair. How was he going to get down from the chair holding the gallon milk container with both hands? He needed a free hand to steady himself as he climbed down. That meant only one thing. He had to hold the milk in one hand. Could he do that? It was pretty heavy and he was barely able to hold on to it with two hands. But he had to try. The baby dinosaur was depending on him.

Steadying his balance, Davy shifted the container to one hand. He then reached out and with his other hand held on to the back of the chair so he could climb down. He stepped off the chair and was half-way down when he heard the skitter-scatter of tiny feet. He looked up and saw the small dinosaur standing in the doorway of the kitchen on its hind legs. Before Davy could stop it, the milk container slipped out of his hands. The container hit the tile floor with a loud "thunk!" A crack opened up on one side of the container and milk spilled out all over the kitchen floor.

Davy stood on the chair looking down as the tiny dinosaur dashed to the side of the small lake of milk and began lapping it up.

"Hey, you. You're not supposed to drink off the floor. Grandma's gonna yell."

Davy climbed down off the chair and knelt down next to the baby *Tyrannosaurus*. It stopped drinking and looked at Davy.

"Well, you must be starving so I guess it's okay. Go on. Drink away."

While the dinosaur resumed drinking, Davy began to play with the milk, drawing in it like he was finger painting. The T.rex looked up from its meal again and saw Davy's finger swirling in the milk. The little animal began mimicking Davy's motion, swirling its tail in the milk. Davy would draw a circle, and so would the tiny T.rex. Davy's eyes couldn't get any wider as he realized the baby dino was playing with him.

"You're a miracle," said Davy. "Now I just have to convince Grandma to let me keep you. They don't allow pets in the building. I know it's a stupid rule. Oh man, if only Mom and Dad could see you! We need a name. What should I call you?"

The little dinosaur looked up at Davy and then at himself.

"Rex. I'll call you Rex," said Davy, smiling.

Down the hall, the door to his grandmother's bedroom opened and Grandma Becky stepped into the hallway, rubbing her eyes as she pulled her bathrobe around her. Fumbling for her glasses, she finally got them on and looked down the hallway. She could see Davy on the floor, but not what he was doing there.

At the same time, a taxi was pulling to the curb right in front of the brownstone. The rear door of the taxi opened and out stepped Professor Berenson.

Back in the kitchen, the tiny dinosaur was drawing a figure eight when it stopped and looked at the surface of the milk, which was moving slightly. What the dinosaur was seeing was the vibration on the surface of the milk caused by Grandma Becky's walking toward the kitchen. The dino looked at Davy, who was oblivious to all this as he continued drawing in the milk. The dino looked at the milk again and noticed the vibrations were getting stronger. Sensing the approach of possible danger, the little creature began running in place, searching for traction on the wet surface. Finally its tiny claws caught an edge of tile and the little beast darted like a shot under the refrigerator just as Grandma Becky's feet appeared on the floor next to Davy's hand. Davy stopped drawing and looked up.

Grandma Becky did not look happy.

"What are you doing?"

She looked at the milk all over the kitchen floor.

"I dropped the milk."

"I can see that. What are you doing in it? Why aren't you cleaning it up?"

"He was scared and I was just trying to get him something to drink."

"Who was scared?"

Davy started to answer when the front door buzzer buzzed.

"Now who could that be on a Sunday morning?" asked Grandma Becky.

As she went to the front door Davy looked around and realized the tiny creature was gone.

"Hey! Now where'd you go?"

Davy looked around the kitchen. He searched under the table and then under the sink. Then he heard a "squeak!" It came from under the refrigerator.

The front door buzzed again.

"Hold on," said Grandma Becky. "I'm coming." She got to the door and looked through the peephole. Shrugging, she unlocked the door and opened it to find Professor Berenson.

"Sorry to bother you, Mrs. Ross. May I come in?"

"Do you have some news about my son and daughter-in-law?"

"No. I'm afraid not. That's not why I'm here."

In the kitchen Davy was looking under the refrigerator when Rex peeked his little head out from under the grating.

"There you are. You're gonna get me in trouble. Now stay put, okay? Grandma will know what to do."

But as soon as Davy gave the order, the dinosaur scurried across the kitchen floor and into the hall. It got halfway down the hallway when it looked up and saw Professor Berenson talking to Grandma Becky.

"It won't take long," pleaded Berenson. "We believe some of the museum's property got mixed in with your son's. If you could just show me where you put that trunk."

Just then Davy entered the hallway on his hands and knees and saw the baby T.rex looking up at the Professor. As Davy began crawling toward it, the dinosaur ran across the hall and back into Davy's bedroom.

"Hey! Wait for me."

Professor Berenson and Grandma Becky both looked down and saw Davy scrambling across the hallway on his hands and knees.

"Davy. Who are you talking to?"

But Davy had already disappeared into his bedroom. Grandma Becky shook her head and turned back toward the Professor.

"He's been acting a little strange ever since, you know."

"I understand completely. If I could just see that trunk now?"

"Of course. It's in the living room," said Grandma Becky.

She led the Professor to the trunk, which was sitting open next to the sofa. The Professor searched through it, tossing clothing and toiletries aside. He let out a deep sigh.

In his bedroom, Davy found Rex in a corner of his closet looking frightened.

"It's okay," said Davy. "Don't be scared. I'll take care of you."

"Davy!" bellowed the sound of Grandma Becky's voice. Davy looked toward the door to his bedroom and then back at the tiny frightened dinosaur trembling in the corner of the closet.

"What is it, Grandma?"

"Professor Berenson would like to talk to you."

Davy put his finger to his mouth to signify quiet. He then noticed the cracked egg on the shelf. He grabbed the egg and shoved it into the closet with Rex, then closed the closet door just as Professor Berenson entered his bedroom uninvited.

"Good morning, Davy."

The Professor noticed the vast number of dinosaur figurines.

"Quite a collection you have here."

A scratching sound could be heard coming from the closet, followed by a faint squeal.

"What was that?" asked Professor Berenson as he walked over to the closet. "Sounds like mice."

Just then, Grandma Becky entered the bedroom.

"Mice? Oh, dear," she said.

Professor Berenson swung open the door to the closet and looked inside. He pushed some clothing aside until he came to the back wall. "Ah-hah," he said, nodding. There was a small hole in the wall down by the floor.

"They're quite harmless, you know," said the Professor, stepping out of the closet.

"You're not a woman, Professor. Women and mice do not co-exist well. I'll have to call the exterminator."

"No!"

Both Grandma Becky and Professor Berenson turned toward the young boy.

"If we have mice, we have to get rid of them," said Grandma Becky.

Davy looked worried.

"Why?"

"We just do."

"Davy," said the Professor. "Not to change the subject, but do you remember the trunk that arrived yesterday? Your grandmother said you were the only other person who might have taken something from it. I'm not talking about the music box. I'm not interested in that, but did you happen to notice anything else? You see, we think something that belongs to the museum might have gotten in there by mistake. You haven't seen anything that looked like it belonged in a museum, have you?"

Davy looked at his grandmother and then at Dr. Berenson.

"You found something, didn't you?" asked the Professor as he knelt down to look Davy in the eye.

"Do I have to give it back?"

Professor Berenson's face lit up. He was unable to contain his enthusiasm. Then he sniffed the air.

"What's that smell?"

Grandma Becky sniffed the air. "Maybe it's those mice."

Professor Berenson turned back toward Davy.

"This something you found? Was it something very special?"

"I was hoping I could keep him."

"Him? Can I see 'him'?"

"I suppose," Davy shrugged. He opened the closet door and knelt down. Reaching deep into the closet, he picked something up. Dr. Berenson's eyes were getting more excited with anticipation. He looked almost gleeful. Then Davy turned around, his hand closed.

"I thought Mom and Dad sent him to me. But if it's yours, I guess you can have it."

"It's best this way, Davy," said the Professor as Davy opened his hand.

You would have thought someone had let the air out of Professor Berenson when he saw it: resting in the palm of Davy's hand was a plastic replica of a *Stegosaurus* in minute detail. Davy reached out and handed it to the Professor.

The Professor stared down at the plastic toy. He realized his mouth was hanging open and immediately closed it. He could feel Davy and Grandma Becky staring at him as he tried to cover his massive disappointment.

"You know, Davy, it's against the law to keep something that doesn't belong to you."

"I don't understand," said Grandma Becky. "He's giving it back to you."

The Professor handed Davy back the toy *Stegosaurus*. "We have so many of these at the museum," he said. "I'm going to let you keep this one."

"What do you say to the Professor, Davy?" said Grandma Becky.

"Thank you," said Davy.

"Well," said the Professor, regaining his composure. "I'd better be going."

The Professor turned and walked out of the brownstone.

Davy went to a bedroom window and climbed up onto the sill to look out. He watched the Professor flag down a taxi. But before he got in, the Professor looked up and gave Davy a stern look. The look sent a chill down Davy's back and he had the feeling the Professor would return.

Davy climbed down from the windowsill and went to his closet and knelt down on the floor.

"That was close. It's all clear. You can come out now," he beckoned.

Rex poked his head out of the mouse hole. Davy reached out and the baby dinosaur scurried into his hand. Davy carried the tiny creature over to his bed.

"You'll be safe with me. I won't let anybody hurt you. Ever."

Davy set Rex down onto his bed.

"You don't want to be in some museum, do you? You'll have more fun with me. But you gotta be quiet."

Davy lay down on his bed next to his new pet, which moved next to Davy and rubbed its tiny head against Davy's hand.

"You'll live here with me and Grandma. How's that sound?"

In the hallway just outside Davy's closed bedroom door, Grandma Becky listened to her grandson talking. She shook her head and walked away.

CHAPTER FIVE

The scent of pancakes toasting on a griddle floated into Davy's bedroom. Rex stuck his head out from under a pillow and sniffed the air. Davy was across the room getting dressed for school.

"Morning, Rex." Davy took in a deep breath. "Pancakes. My favorite. Don't worry. I'll save you some."

Davy entered the kitchen and found his grandmother in her nurse's uniform standing over a hot griddle, flipping a blueberry pancake. He set his backpack on an empty chair and sat down at his placemat at the far end of the table.

"Morning, Grandma," he said, taking a sip of orange juice. He was about to take another sip when he saw something move inside his backpack. Something was inside pushing against the fabric. Davy put down his juice and arranged the backpack so his grandmother could not see the movement.

"How many pancakes can you eat?"

"Three," said Davy, and then looked at the backpack. "Better make it four."

"Four? You must be hungry."

Grandma Becky put three pancakes on a plate and set them in front of her grandson. "Start on these while I make some more." She went back to the griddle and poured more batter on the hot surface.

"I'm going to be taking care of a former ambassador to what used to be called Yugoslavia today. I want you to give these telephone numbers to your homeroom teacher in case the school has to reach me. I should be done by the time you get home. How do I look?"

"You look fine, Grandma. Why?"

"Well, he's a widower. You never know. I want to look my best."

She carried another pancake over to the table. "Eat your breakfast. I have to finish getting ready for work."

Grandma Becky removed her apron and left the kitchen. As soon as she was gone, Davy took the fourth pancake off the plate with a fork, opened the top of his backpack, and dropped the pancake inside. He then put his ear next to the opening and listened to munching sounds.

Grandma Becky walked Davy the six blocks to school and when they got there, she gave him some money for lunch.

"Did you remember to bring something for your science project?"

"I'm all set," smiled Davy. As he said it, something moved inside his backpack again.

"I think your project is moving," said Grandma Becky. "What do you have in there?"

"Huh?" said Davy. "I must have left it turned on by mistake. I'd better shut it off before the batteries run down."

Davy reached into his backpack and stroked Rex's head gently.

"There," he said. "That's better."

Grandma Becky bent down and kissed Davy on the cheek. "I'll see you after school."

"Bye, Grandma."

She watched as he ran toward the entrance of the public school along with a group of other children. Just before he disappeared inside, something moved inside the backpack again.

"Davy!" she shouted. But he had already gone inside. "Oh, well. Time to go see Mr. Former Ambassador." She straightened her uniform, patted her hair, and headed off down the street.

In the third period science classroom, Mrs. Howard tried to bring some kind of order to the chaos that had taken over her sixth grade class. This seemed to happen whenever she assigned a special science project. Maybe she should write a paper for an education journal and title it, "A Chaos Theory of Science Project Day."

"Okay, children. Take your seats," said Mrs. Howard, who at 55 still dressed like a hippie. Today she was wearing a long denim dress and moccasins.

"I know how excited everyone is about showing off their projects, but we can't start until everyone is in their seats. Davy. Gretchen. Edgar. That means you."

Reluctantly, the children put away their various projects and took their seats. Davy sat in front of Gretchen. He checked his chair first to make sure she hadn't put something on it before he sat down. Last week, she'd managed to sneak a big wad of bubble gum on there just as he took his seat. She smiled at Davy as he slowly turned and took his seat.

Gretchen was bored already. How was she going to last the whole day with these babies? At 12, Gretchen was older than most other sixth graders. She started school a year later than the rest of them because her mother had moved to the city too late to begin the year before.

She stared out the window at the park as she took her seat behind Davy. That's where I should be, she thought. But then something incredible grabbed her attention.

She had just settled into her chair when she found herself face to face with a tiny creature stretching its head out from under the top flap of Davy Ross's backpack.

"Whoa," said Gretchen. "What have we here?"

She reached out with her finger to touch the little animal when it pulled its head back inside.

A faint whimpering sound came from the backpack and Davy turned around. Gretchen smiled at him and raised her hand.

"Yes, Gretchen."

"Mrs. Howard. I think Davy should go first."

Davy glared at Gretchen and she stuck her tongue out at him.

"And just why do you think that, Gretchen?"

"Well, from what I can tell, Davy brought another dinosaur to class."

"Davy?" said Mrs. Ross. "Is Gretchen right?"

Davy suddenly looked very nervous.

"Come on, Davy. We have a lot of work to get through today," said Mrs. Howard. "I have to say I'm a little disappointed. I was hoping you'd gotten over this obsession with dinosaurs, but if we have to see another one, let's have it."

Davy let out a sigh and stood up. He looked at Gretchen and reached inside his backpack.

"Mrs. Howard," said Davy as his hand found the baby dinosaur. "I think I should warn you. He's a little scared so don't make any sudden moves, okay?"

Mrs. Howard shook her head, smiling. "Oh, I'll try."

"He's just a baby," explained Davy. Then he turned his head toward the backpack and spoke down into it with a soothing, calm voice. "Come on out. It's okay. This is my school."

Mrs. Howard rolled her eyes and looked at her watch. Some of the other children began to giggle.

"Okay, Davy. That's enough. Just show us the dinosaur already," snapped Mrs. Howard.

Davy pulled his hand out of the backpack with the tiny dinosaur in the palm of his hand. Holding his hand flat and out in front of him, he walked to the front of the class.

Mrs. Howard wasn't really paying attention until Davy held his hand out in front of her face.

She did a double-take and then moved in closer.

"It looks so real. I'm impressed Davy. You've outdone yourself. Now, do you want to tell us something about this one?"

Gretchen stood up. "Mrs. Howard, it *is* real. I saw it move."

"That'll be enough, Gretchen. You'll have your turn. Now please sit down. Go ahead, Davy. What kind is this? It looks like some kind of *Tyrannosaurus*."

Davy held the tiny dinosaur up so the entire class could see. Meanwhile, Mrs. Howard put her glasses on and bent in closer to examine the details on what she assumed was a painted figurine.

"I call him Rex," said Davy. "He was born yesterday in my bedroom. Or at least that's where he hatched."

As Davy spoke, Mrs. Howard's eyes squinted as she bent in to take a closer look.

"He looks so real," she said. "It's amazing. The detail. Where did you get—"

But before she could finish her sentence, Rex turned his head and looked Mrs. Howard right in the eye.

"Aggghhhh!" she screamed, jerking her head back. "What is that thing? It's alive!"

"It's my dinosaur."

"What is that, some kind of lizard? A live lizard! I will not have a live lizard in my classroom."

"But Mrs. Howard—"

"Get it out of here. Now!"

Mrs. Howard grabbed Davy by the arm and started to lead him toward the door when Rex leaped off Davy's hand onto the teacher's shoulder, across her back, onto her desk, and into an open drawer.

"Oh, God. It was on me. Where'd it go?"

"It's in your desk."

"Get it out of there."

Davy ran to the desk and opened the drawer. He saw Rex hiding in a corner, looking scared, shaking.

"It's okay, Rex. Don't hurt him, Mrs. Howard."

"Just get it out of my desk!"

Davy reached in and Rex crawled into Davy's hand. Davy carried Rex back to his backpack, opened the flap and placed him inside. He then closed the flap so Rex couldn't get out.

Mrs. Howard put a hand to her forehead.

"I'm sorry Mrs. Howard," said Davy.

"That's okay Davy. I can understand how this must be a difficult time for you. But I thought I made it clear. No live animals."

"I know. But I just thought ..."

"I'm afraid I'm going to have to call your Grandmother to come get it."

"No. Please. Don't do that. I won't let him out," pleaded Davy. "I promise."

"Oh Davy. Okay. Let's continue. Who's next?"

CHAPTER SIX

Later that night, the Professor strolled the halls of the Natural History Museum. The museum had closed hours ago and this was the Professor's favorite time in the museum, when it was just him and hundreds of stuffed and mounted animals. He stood in the great hall of dinosaurs, looking up at the towering skeletons of the giant creatures. He had a perplexed look on his face as he walked closer to the skeleton of a *Triceratops*. He reached out touched the hipbone. He leaned in closer and took a deep whiff.

"You're losing it Berenson. Fossils don't have a smell," he said to himself. "But I know something else that does."

The Professor ran back to his office and turned on a light. His office was filled with files and fossils ready to be classified. He strode across the office and picked up one of the bones from Sam's backpack. He put the bone to his nose and sniffed again.

"That's it. I knew I recognized the smell. Davy, you little devil."

The Professor's mouth broke into a wide smile as he sniffed the bone again as if it contained an elegant perfume.

The taxi moved slowly down the deserted street in the Soho district of lower Manhattan, passing lofts, art galleries, and warehouses. The driver was looking at numbers on buildings, searching for an address. The taxi lurched to a stop in front of a building that looked like an old factory. The back door of the taxi opened and out stepped the Professor, who looked up at the refurbished factory building. He waited for the taxi to drive away before crossing the street and entering the old building.

The Professor rode an open elevator to the top floor. He was holding something inside his coat. When he reached the top, he took out the bone he had sniffed in his office. He sniffed it again for good measure. The elevator stopped at a door and the Professor knocked.

"Who's there?" questioned a man's voice from the other side of the door.

"Jackson. Open the door. It's me." The door opened and the Professor entered. "You may not have to make that trip back to Africa after all."

"In that case," said Jackson, closing the door behind the Professor and then going to a table where he picked up the envelope the Professor had given him in the museum, "you might as well take this back before I spend it."

Jackson stood there, half-dressed and yawning, and holding out the envelope but the Professor ignored him and instead pulled out the bone.

"Keep it, Jackson. I've got another job for you. Come over here. I want you to smell something."

The following night, Davy and Grandma Becky were in the supermarket when someone broke into their apartment. The tiny dinosaur was sleeping under Davy's pillow when it heard the sound. He stuck his head out of the covers and saw a shadow sweep across the bedroom window. He then saw a gloved hand cut an opening in the glass windowpane. There was now a perfect circle cut in the glass. Suddenly, the gloved hand reached in through the hole and unlatched the window. Two hands pushed the window up and a man slipped into the room. There was some light coming from the hallway so the tiny dinosaur could see the man's face. It was Jackson, but the little creature didn't know that. It just knew danger was in the room and it kept very still and very quiet as Jackson began searching the apartment.

About an hour later, Davy and his grandmother were walking home from the store. Grandma Becky was pushing a shopping cart full of groceries and Davy was acting out a death match between Jesse the Body Ventura and a *Stegosaurus*. Jesse was winning.

"That was a mean trick you played on Mrs. Howard," said Grandma Becky.

"I still think she over-reacted a bit," said Davy. "Other kids have brought pets to school."

"But you don't have any pets. They told me it was some kind of lizard. What happened to it, anyway? You didn't bring it home, did you?"

"Of course not. I set it free in the park."

"How did I ever let you talk me into buying all this food? You're never going to drink this much milk. It'll just go bad."

"But, Grandma. You're always telling me to drink more milk, aren't you?"

"I suppose I should be glad you got your appetite back," she said as she got out her keys and unlocked the front door to the apartment.

As soon as Davy and Grandma stepped inside, they realized someone had been in the apartment. The place was a mess. At first Davy thought maybe Rex had gone a little stir crazy, but Rex couldn't turn over a sofa or upend a bookcase.

"Oh, dear. I think we've been robbed," said Grandma Becky. "I'd better call the police."

Davy ran to his bedroom, which was completely torn apart. Toys were thrown everywhere. So were Davy's clothes. His closet was completely empty. Who would do that? Oh, no. What about Rex? Davy looked at his bed. The mattress was on the floor. His pillows were torn apart.

"Rex!" shouted Davy.

A scratching sound came from overhead. Davy looked up at the glass shield under the light and saw the outline of a tiny dinosaur.

"There you are." He stood on his bed and reached up. Rex crawled to the edge of the light and then dropped down onto Davy's hand.

"You poor little fella. Did you see who did this?"

Ten blocks away, Professor Berenson was sitting at his desk in the Natural History Museum when Jackson entered and approached the desk. He reached in the pocket of his long leather coat and pulled out the egg-shaped object. He set it down on the desk in front of the Professor.

"What's this?" asked the Professor.

53

"Take a whiff," said Jackson, smiling.

The Professor picked up the egg and sniffed it. He poked a pencil inside and peered into the empty shell. He put the egg back down and turned toward Jackson.

"That's what was causing the smell. I tore the place apart before I found it. The boy had it hidden in his closet."

"Do you know what this is?" asked the Professor.

"Stink bomb?"

"It's an egg."

"What kind of animal lays eggs like that?"

"The kind that's not supposed to be around anymore."

"Whatta ya mean, Professor?"

The Professor picked up the egg and inspected it again closely.

"This, my good man, is a dinosaur egg."

"No kidding."

"Unfortunately, it's empty."

"Well, yeah. It must be few million years old, right?"

The Professor walked over to a window and looked out into the night.

"That egg just hatched, Jackson."

"No. You can't be serious. You're telling me that a baby dinosaur is loose in New York City?"

"Maybe. Maybe not loose exactly."

"Just what this city needs. Something else to worry about."

"You think I'm joking."

"You're either joking or you're crazy."

"The egg is empty. Whatever was inside is gone."

"And if that's a dinosaur egg then whatever was inside is long gone and long dead."

"If that's so, Jackson, then why is the inside of the shell still damp and sticky?"

"I don't know, but if this is a real dinosaur egg," said Jackson, picking it up, "I know a collector who'll give you $250,000 for it."

Professor Berenson took the egg away from Jackson. "I don't want to sell this one just yet."

"You're the boss," said Jackson.

CHAPTER SEVEN

A week had passed since the egg hatched. A Happy Birthday sign was strung across the entrance to the living room of the apartment. Davy blew out all eleven candles on his birthday cake and gave his grandmother a kiss on the cheek.

"I'm sorry it wasn't more of a party," said Grandma Becky.

"It was fine, Grandma."

"I told you to invite some of your friends from school."

"That's okay. I'm fine," insisted Davy. "Besides, we had a party in class so they already wished me happy birthday. This was great, Grandma, honest. I'm gonna go do my homework now. Do you think I could take an extra piece of cake to my room for later?"

"Sure, Davy," she said, and cut him another piece of chocolate cake.

"Davy?"

"Yes, Grandma."

"I'm worried about you. I never see you playing with any of the other kids. You don't seem to have any friends."

"I'm okay, Grandma. Besides, I do have a friend."

"You do? What's his name?"

"Rex."

"How come you never have Rex over?"

"I usually go over there. He's got a lot of cool video games."

"Davy. I'm sorry."

"Don't worry, Grandma," said Davy. "I'm fine."

Davy took the cake to his room and closed the door. He went to his desk and opened one of the deeper drawers where he had made up a little home for Rex.

Rex crawled out of the drawer and onto the desk. Davy pushed the plate of cake toward the little creature, who was now twice as big as it was when it hatched, which meant it was now about twelve inches tall, or the size of a large action figure.

"This can be your birthday, too."

Rex began to devour the cake. When he was finished, he burped a little burp. Davy picked him up and carried him over to his bed.

"I'm afraid I can't take you to school anymore. So, you're gonna have to learn to stay here on your own. But it'll be okay. I'll leave the TV on so you'll have something to do. And I'll leave some food out. Okay? Are we partners?"

Davy put out a finger and Rex touched it with a tiny claw.

"Partners," said Davy.

During the next week, Davy noticed that Rex was growing pretty fast. In fact, he was getting too big to hide in the bedroom. There used to be a pigeon coop on the roof so Davy checked to see if it was still there. The wood was rotting and the sides were starting to fall apart, but it appeared to be vacant. It would have to do, at least until Rex outgrew it.

The baby tyranno was now already two feet tall. His size had doubled in the last few days and his appetite seemed to quadruple. He could go through food faster than a dozen cats. Davy didn't know how he was going to keep feeding him at this rate. Plus, Grandma Becky was getting suspicious. Davy found that out when he overheard her talking.

"You wouldn't believe how much the boy eats," she said to someone one the phone. "He must have one of those high metabolisms because he eats enough for three people."

Just then, a two-foot tall *Tyrannosaurus* ran from the hall into a bedroom. Grandma Becky's mouth dropped open.

"Excuse me a second." She lowered the receiver of the phone as she stared into the hallway. "I must be seeing things again," she said to herself.

At that moment, Davy appeared, holding a remote-control device. Grandma Becky smiled and sighed. "Thank God. It's only Davy and some kind of toy."

She put the phone back to her ear.

"I'm sorry. Where was I. Oh, yes, he eats and eats and doesn't even get fat. I just look at a bagel and put on ten pounds."

Later that night, Davy and Rex were up on the roof looking at pictures of places where Davy's parents had traveled on their digs. "They've gone all over the world," said Davy, as he turned another page.

Rex looked down and put his foot on the page, right on top of a mountain peak.

"Move your foot, Rex."

Davy nudged the dinosaur's foot aside when Rex didn't respond. Underneath where the foot had been were the words, "Mount Kilimanjaro."

"Do you know where this is?"

Rex tapped his foot on the picture and then bent his head down and with his little tongue, licked the picture. "Wow," said Davy. Suddenly a thought exploded in his mind. "Rex, do you think you could find this place?"

Rex nudged Davy's hand with his nose. Davy studied the caption. It said Mount Kilimanjaro was Africa's highest mountain peak. It was located on the border of Tazmania and Kenya.

"Africa," said Davy. "How are we going to get to Africa?"

Over the next few days, Davy downloaded everything he could about Africa from the Internet. Meanwhile, Rex continued to get bigger and bigger. In fact, he was now too big for the chicken coop. He was nearly a foot taller than Davy.

"Time to find you a new home, pal," said Davy, as he led the five-foot tall dinosaur down the back alley behind the apartment building. They got to the street and Davy looked both ways before feeling safe enough to cross without being seen. With the coast clear, Davy and Rex ran across Central Park West and into the park.

They passed a bearded man trying to find a comfortable position on a park bench without spilling his half-empty bottle of something in a bag. The man looked up at Davy and frowned.

"You're supposed to have that dinosaur on a leash," the old man snorted.

"Okay," answered Davy, rushing past. "Thanks."

Davy shook his head and continued on into the park. The night was clear and a nearly full moon lighted their way.

"Ya know, Grandma told me never to go out in the park at night, because it wasn't safe, but it looks pretty safe to me," said Davy. "Before we get to your new home, I want to show you my favorite place. It's just over there."

They walked through a playground of swings and sandboxes to a large mound. Built into the side of the mound was a huge slide.

"We stopped coming because of the rats," said Davy. "Look, there they are, under the slide. I hate those rats. They scared all the kids away so now nobody can go down the slide."

Rex looked up at the slide and smiled. He scrambled up the rocky side of the mound and when he got to the top, he sat on the slide and slid down in a whoosh! "Rex! Watch out!"

Suddenly, rats began swarming out of every rock and crevice, surrounding Rex, who landed in a thump at the foot of the slide. The rats bared their little teeth and began to snap at Rex, who merely shrugged, then lashed out and grabbed the biggest rat of all and tossed him in his mouth like a piece of popcorn. Chomp! Gulp! Crunch! Swallow! No more rat. The other rats just stared at Rex for a second before they realized any one of them could be the next course, and they scattered in every direction. In less than a moment, the slide was rat-free and Rex was looking back at the top. He nodded to Davy to follow him and up they went.

Using Rex like a sled, Davy sat across his stomach and they slid down the slide together, going faster than Davy had ever gone before.

"Wow," said Davy when they reached the bottom. "That was incredible."

Rex was ready to go again, but Davy shook his head. "I want to go again, too, but we have to go. We'll come back. I promise."

They walked south until they came to Central Park South. Near the public entrance to the subway there was a separate doorway used by maintenance crews. Davy had found it on one of his house-hunting missions to find Rex a better place to stay.

He led Rex down into the subway shaft until they came to a spot where some homeless people had left a mattress and other odds and ends.

"Don't worry," said Davy. "Nobody lives here anymore. I figure this will be good for a while, but if you keep growing, you won't be here long. I brought some food and there are some cans of Spam under the mattress. You're gonna be okay here, right?"

Just then a rat scrambled along the wall and into the darkness. Rex followed it with his eyes and looked back at Davy. "Rats. Well, that should solve your food problem. Okay. I'm gonna go now. But I'll be back tomorrow after school. You have to promise me you won't go outside."

Rex nodded.

"Good boy."

Davy felt bad about leaving Rex alone in a subway shaft, but he didn't think he had any other choice. He knew, by now, that Rex would do almost anything Davy told him to do. So he felt confident that Rex would be there when he came back. The encounter in the park with the wino convinced Davy that he had to come up with some way to disguise his new friend.

The next night, when Davy came by to take Rex for a walk, he brought something with him: one of his father's raincoats and a wide-brimmed hat. The coat barely covered Rex, and that hat looked silly, but from a distance, it was just enough to make it appear that an old man with a hump back was walking with a boy.

Over the next few days, Rex continued to grow about two inches a day. Before long, he was too big for the coat and had to stoop inside the subway airshaft. Seeing how uncomfortable it was for Rex really bothered Davy.

"I'm afraid you're gonna have to stay here a little while longer," said Davy, as he led him back into the airshaft.

Rex just grunted.

"Just until I can figure out a better place to hide you, okay?"

Rex nodded and sighed as he squeezed into the airshaft and disappeared into the darkness.

At school the next day, Davy saw a poster for Dino "The Dinosaur" Donato, one of Davy's favorite wrestlers. According to the poster, Dino was coming to New York for the annual Halloween Parade. Last year, Dino had put on a benefit match to raise money for Davy's school library. The school had praised the wrestler for single-handedly inspiring an entire class of fifth grade boys to read books by writing an autobiography.

Dino's signature move was the "T-Wrecks," where he would swing his opponent over his shoulder and then spin him around before slamming him into the mat.

All day long, Davy fantasized about what a match would be like between Dino and a real dinosaur. Now that really would be something to see.

That night, Davy was heading for his room about to pretend he was getting ready for bed when Grandma Becky stopped him. "Davy. I want to talk to you."

Davy turned toward his grandmother, wondering if she had somehow discovered his nightly excursions.

"Yes, Grandma."

"Here," she said, handing him a photo album. She opened it for him and he saw pictures of his mother and father when they were younger. There were even some pictures of his Dad as a young boy.

"I thought you might want to have these," she said sadly.

"Are you sure, Grandma?" asked Davy.

"I'm sure, Davy. I've had these pictures all my life and they are forever imprinted in here," she said pointing to her head. "So I'm passing them along to you, so you'll always have a record of your parents. Sometimes our memories fade, and these will remind you as time goes on."

"Okay, Grandma," said Davy, "but that won't have to happen because I'm gonna see my parents again. They're just waiting for somebody to find them."

"I pray to God you're right, Davy. I really do."

"Never hurts to pray, Grandma. I'm gonna go do my homework and go to sleep. Thanks for the pictures." Davy kissed his Grandma on the cheek and went to his room.

Inside his bedroom, he locked the door and listened for his grandmother. Not hearing anything, he went to the window, opened it, and climbed out on to the fire escape, carrying a brown bag of leftovers from dinner.

When he reached the ground, Davy made sure no one was watching before he ran down the alley next to his building, then across the street and into the park.

He ran most of the way to Central Park South and the subway airshaft. Looking around again to see if anyone was paying any attention to him, he entered the airshaft. Inside, there was an old open-door elevator. He stepped on the elevator and hit a button. The elevator began its squeaky descent into the darkness under the city streets, deep beneath the subway and sewer tunnels into a damp netherworld of manmade caverns and tunnels.

A tremor of fear rippled down his back. What if Rex wasn't here, he wondered? His grandmother was always warning him about going into the park alone, even during the day. And now here he was at night, going beneath the park alone. He could feel his heart racing.

The elevator stopped and Davy got off. The ground around him began to shake as a subway train rushed past nearby.

Davy took a deep breath and tried to shake off the anxiety that filled his body. He kept remembering something his father once said. "Fear can be a good thing, Davy. Fear can keep you alert and alive."

This was a scary looking place with its dimly lit tunnels and dripping water. Davy was trembling as he reached into an ugly hole in the wall to retrieve a giant flashlight that he had stored there for his visits.

Holding the flashlight in one hand and the bag of leftovers in the other, Davy walked slowly down a tunnel completely devoid of light, except for what the flashlight gave off. The walls of the tunnel looked like they were sweating in this damp, dank underground road.

He hadn't walked very far when he heard a crunching sound, and then another. It was the sound of a very heavy foot, and something scraping stone.

"Rex?"

Davy now started to feel a little frightened. What if someone else was down here? What if the people who owned the mattresses had decided to come back?

"Rex? That you, buddy?" he said, as he walked a little farther. "I brought you some food."

Behind him and out the shadows extended a large reptilian hand. The hand grabbed Davy from behind and lifted him off the floor.

"Agghhh!"

Davy looked real scared now as he found himself carried through the air and around to the face in the beam of the flashlight, the giant head of a *Tyrannosaurus rex* with a hungry look in his eyes.

Rex now stood just over six and a half feet tall. His mouth was full of large, stained teeth. Back on the ground again, Davy tossed some food up into the open mouth, which received it eagerly. Davy tried to smile as Rex ate the food in one gulp.

"Rex! You've gotten bigger. I should have brought some more food."

Rex snorted and looked Davy up and down as if he offered a more filling meal.

"Hey. Don't look at me like that."

Rex picked Davy up again and began to smell him.

"Put me down."

But Rex licked his lips and started to bring Davy close to his mouth when Davy made a face.

"Rex, your breath stinks. You've been eating rats again, haven't you?"

Rex tilted his head and then sort of shrugged as he put Davy down on the floor of the tunnel.

"Stop looking at me like dessert. Are you ready for your walk?"

Rex nodded his head up and down like an excited puppy waiting to go outside.

"Okay, but no fooling around this time."

Rex gave Davy a crooked grin, or as much of a grin a *T.rex* could manage, and then started to walk off down a different tunnel.

"Hey! Where are you going?"

Rex nodded for Davy to follow him and he did. They went through an elaborate set of tunnels under the East River, coming out on an uninhabited end of Roosevelt Island.

"Where are we?" asked Davy as he looked around at a place he had never been before. He looked across the river at the Manhattan Skyline. "Is this New Jersey?"

Rex was jumping up and down and encouraging Davy to follow him some more. Rex ran off and Davy chased behind until they came to a playground with mazes and monkey bars, and forts and big swings. Davy stood before the playground in awe. "Wow."

He then ran to one of the swings and tried to get it going but it was too hard. "I could use a push here," said Davy. Rex lumbered behind him and gave him a mighty shove, sending Davy up as far as the swing would go without going over the bar.

A few hundred yards away, two policemen were parked under the 59th Street Bridge taking a coffee break.

One of the officers was sprinkling some artificial sweetener into his coffee when he looked toward the playground. He then dropped his coffee in his lap.

"Aggghhhh! That's hot."

"What's the matter with you?" asked his partner.

"Did you see that?"

"See what?"

"I must be losing it," said the policeman who spilled his coffee.

"You certainly lost your coffee."

"You didn't see it."

His partner just stared at him.

"You're gonna think I'm nuts, but I swore I saw a dinosaur pushing some kid on a swing over on that playground."

His partner continued to stare at him and then glanced over toward the playground, which was now empty.

"We'll be back on days next week. It's these night shifts. They can drive ya loony."

"Yeah," agreed his partner.

Davy and Rex, wearing the raincoat and hat disguise, had finished playing and were making their way back to the subway tunnel to return to Manhattan.

"That was fun, Rex, but we have some work to do."

Rex gave Davy a curious look.

"You're getting too big for the sewer."

Rex nodded in agreement.

"You're also outgrowing that raincoat. We're going back to Central Park. I found a spot under the park where you'll be able to stay for another foot or so. It's also near the big slide."

Rex clapped his claws together.

"Thought you'd like that."

After walking for nearly an hour, Davy and Rex came out of the subway tunnel near the park. They had just begun heading toward the big slide when they heard the first scream.

Rex looked toward where the sound came from and began walking in that direction with Davy behind him.

"Help! Please! Somebody!"

It was a woman's voice.

"Somebody's in trouble," said Davy.

Rex looked at Davy for some guidance when they heard another cry.

"No. Don't!" pleaded the woman.

"Come on," said Davy. "Let's check it out."

They quietly peeked through the bushes next to a path running alongside a small pond. On the bank next to the path, they could see three attackers pulling at a woman in jogging clothes.

"Please. Don't hurt me," she begged.

"Stop kicking and we won't," said one of the attackers.

Just then Rex stepped on a twig and it snapped.

"Shhh. I think I heard something," said another, looking around.

"Come on," said the third attacker. "Let's get it over with."

From his hiding spot, Davy could see the woman's face. She looked very scared as she stared up at one of the attackers who was now standing over her. She closed her eyes mouthed a silent prayer. Davy turned toward Rex, but Rex was gone. He looked back at the woman just as she opened her eyes and let out a scream, "Agggghhh!"

"Hey! Take it easy lady. I ain't gonna kill ya," said the attacker standing over her. But then he realized the woman wasn't even looking at him, but over his shoulder. He turned around just in time to see one of his friends lifted off his feet and tossed into the bushes.

"What the ...."

But before he could get out all the words, the third attacker was being pulled into the bushes by some unseen force and hurled into the nearby pond with a splash.

"Will you guys stop fooling around? We got work to do," he said looking back toward the woman. He reached down for a pouch that was attached to a belt around her waist when something grabbed the back of his jacket. It pulled him up and away from the woman. The attacker looked down as he saw his feet leave the ground.

"Hey!" he shouted as he began to kick at whatever was holding him off the ground and carrying him toward a wire mesh trashcan.

The woman stopped screaming and realized her attacker was no longer standing over her. She started to sit up when she saw what appeared to be a *Tyrannosaurus rex* drop the assailant into the trashcan. She took a deep breath, blinked and looked again.

This time Rex looked back at her and nodded. The woman opened her mouth to speak, but no words came out. Instead, she fainted into unconsciousness. Davy ran to her from the bushes, knelt down and felt her pulse.

"She seems okay," said Davy. "Guess *you* scared her more than the muggers."

The sound of police sirens could be heard in the background.

"Somebody must have called the cops," said Davy. "Let's get out of here!"

CHAPTER EIGHT

A few days later, Professor Berenson sat in his office at the museum going through a stack of newspapers. He looked tired and rubbed his eyes, as he continued going through the pile of papers on the desk in front of him.

He was drawing circles around some of the headlines.

"Police Baffled over Drop in Crime in Central Park."

"Muggers Afraid to Enter Park at Night."

"Monster Stalks Park After Dark."

"Jogger Claims Giant Creature Chased Off Attackers."

"Rat Population Going Down in City."

"Are Rats Fleeing to Suburbs?"

"Big Slide in Park Safe Again."

The Professor opened a desk drawer and reached inside. He removed the egg and looked at it.

"So you've grown into quite a little mischief maker," he said, talking to the empty eggshell. "Oh, Davy. You've done a spectacular job. Your parents would be proud."

The Professor set down the egg and picked up the phone.

"Michael, my boy," he said to someone into the phone. "I may be coming into possession of something that would fit quite nicely in your collection. I know you only collect animals that are extinct. This one definitely meets your criteria. However, I'm afraid the price is going to be a little steep. Ten million. Don't tell me you can't afford it. My dear boy, if I told you what it was you wouldn't believe me. I'd much rather show you. When? Soon. I'll be in touch."

The Professor hung up the phone and picked up one of the newspapers and smiled.

That night, back in Central Park, Davy and Rex were taking one of their evening walks.

"I think I found the perfect place for you to live. One that should last more than a couple of days, too."

They stopped in front of large body of water right in the middle of the park.

"Its a rowing pond," said Davy. "And guess what? See that big rock out there?"

Rex looked at the rock in the middle of the lake. "Under that rock," continued Davy, "is a big cave. I read about it in a book about Central Park. That's gonna be your new home."

Rex shook his head "no."

"Why not?" asked Davy.

Rex nodded "no" again and began to walk away.

"Hey, wait. Where are you going?"

Rex began walking under a grove of trees and Davy ran to catch up.

"What's the matter? Is it the water? Are you afraid of the water?"

Rex gave Davy a sheepish smile.

"That's it. You don't know if you're able to swim. I'll just have to show you."

As they walked along, Davy looked up at the trees and shook his head. Rex looked up, too, as they continued along the path.

"I know. I feel it, too," said Davy. "We're being watched. I only hope whatever is watching us has four legs."

Davy continued walking beneath the grove of trees, looking up every now and then, hoping to spot whatever was spying on them from above. He thought he detected some movement high in the trees. It was as if whatever was watching them was following them from above, moving from tree to tree through the branches.

Davy stopped under a wide oak tree and Rex came up alongside him.

"Something's definitely up there," said Davy, looking up. Rex looked up into the tree and turned his head slightly. He sniffed the air and then snarled. Suddenly a squirrel scurried down the side of the tree, startling both Davy and Rex.

"Agggh!" screamed Davy. "A squirrel. It was a squirrel."

Rex shook his head and snorted a laugh.

"You think it's funny, huh? You won't think it's so funny if someone actually sees you. They'll have you drugged and caged before you can say *Pterodactyl*."

Rex lowered his head.

"That's better," said Davy. "We've come this far. I can't lose you now. That Professor from the museum has been coming around the apartment some more so we have to be real careful."

Davy picked up a flat stone and threw it out across the boat pond, watching it skip, skip, skip across. Suddenly, Rex looked back up into the tree and sniffed the air.

"What is it? More squirrels?" Davy asked, looking up into the high branches.

"Just don't go chasing squirrels on me," said Davy.

Rex squatted and then, with his powerful back legs, leaped up and landed on a thick branch of a tree. Using his strong rear legs, he shimmied up the trunk, through the higher branches.

"What did I just say?" asked Davy.

Rex ignored Davy and climbed higher into the tree.

"Rex. Get down here now!"

Rex was near the top when he reached a platform wedged between two branches. Sitting on the platform was a young girl.

"Rex! Did you hear me?" shouted Davy.

The girl stared at the large head of the dinosaur in disbelief. Rex tilted his head and snorted. He then reached out with one of his small arms, causing the girl to lose her balance.

"Aggghhh!" she screamed as she fell from the platform. Fortunately, the lower branches and leaves broke her fall and she landed on soft thick patch of grass beneath the tree.

Davy rushed over to her as Rex climbed down the tree behind him.

"Gretchen?" said Davy as he recognized the girl from his science class. "Gretchen Tucker?"

Gasping for the breath that had been knocked out of her from the fall, she opened her eyes and looked up.

"Davy Ross?"

She starrted to sit up but then she saw Rex lumbering toward her. "Get that thing away from me."

"Maybe you should wait over there," Davy said to Rex, nodding toward the tree. Rex put his head down and walked back to the tree.

Gretchen followed Rex with her frightened eyes. Rex shook his head and hid behind the tree.

"What is it?" asked Gretchen.

"Don't be scared," said Davy, kneeling down next to her. "What were you doing up in that tree?"

"None of your business."

"I'll make a deal with you, Gretchen," said Davy, standing up with her. "I won't tell anyone about you being in the trees if you won't tell anyone what you saw."

Rex was now hiding behind the tree and out of sight.

"What exactly did I see?"

"You promise me you won't scream?"

"Why would I scream?"

"Rex, come on out."

Rex stepped out from behind the tree, looking sheepish.

Gretchen got up and stood behind Davy.

"He won't hurt you. You're not gonna tell anyone, are you?"

Gretchen shook her head. "Besides, who'd believe me?"

"This is Rex." Rex walked over to Gretchen and Davy, but Gretchen backed away.

"He just wants to smell you," explained Davy.

"Smell me?"

"He can tell whether you're a friend or an enemy from your smell."

"What if he doesn't like my smell?"

"Don't worry. I can tell. He likes you."

"How can you be so sure?"

"Because he hasn't eaten you yet."

Rex walked over to Gretchen and stuck his head down next to her.

"Stop that," she commanded.

Rex put his nose against Gretchen's arm.

She backed away.

"Okay. That's enough, Rex."

Rex backed away.

"You got a leash for that thing?"

"Hear that, Rex? She's the second person to say you should be on a leash."

Rex growled his displeasure.

"It was a joke," said Gretchen. "Is he what I think he is?"

"What do you think he is?"

"A din... a dino... I can't believe I'm even saying it. A dinosaur?"

"A dinosaur? You think Rex is a dinosaur?"

"Okay, you got me. What is he? One of those South American giant lizards or something?"

"No, actually, you were right the first time. He's a baby *Tyrannosaurus*."

Gretchen nodded to herself. "Oh, I'm sure. A baby?"

"Remember the thing I brought to school?"

"That's it? Oh my God. How did it get so big so soon?"

"My dad says dinosaurs may be related to the bird family and birds grow pretty fast. At least that's the theory. Nobody really knows how fast dinosaurs grow."

"Dinosaurs are extinct, Davy. This must be some kind of giant dragon lizard or something. I've seen them on the Discovery Channel. They come from New Zealand or something. Kimino Dragons. They can grow to be 20 feet long."

"I think Rex is gonna be bigger than that," said Davy.

"Aren't you kinda young to be out in the park alone?" asked Gretchen.

Davy looked at Rex. "I'm not alone."

"Oh, yeah. Right."

"What about you? What were you doing up in the tree?"

"It's kind of hard to explain. It's better if I show you. Come on. Follow me."

Davy and Rex started to follow Gretchen when she stopped and turned around.

"Can we leave him here?"

"Stay here, Rex. I'll be right back."

Gretchen scrambled up the big oak tree like a spider monkey. She got to the first branch and then reached down to pull Davy up. Once on the lower branch, he was able to follow her through a maze of natural branch pathways between the trees. They went through elaborate structures of rooms and hallways, made without nails or unnatural material, using branches, twigs and leaves.

"Wow!" said Davy. "You did this?"

"I made sure nothing I did hurt the trees. No nails. No cuts. Everything is built into the trees naturally."

"You live here? Are you some kind of tree sprite?"

77

"What's a tree sprite?"

Davy looked down and saw Rex following them on the ground. "I don't know," he said. "I heard it somewhere in a story or something. What do you do up here?"

"Lots of things. My mother works nights, so she doesn't care. I like to watch people. I'd rather be up here than home alone, zoned out in front of a TV or computer screen."

"Really? I don't see too many people around."

"All right. We had our TV repossessed and we never had a computer."

"I don't live too far from here," said Davy. "You wanta come watch TV with me?"

"That's okay," said Gretchen. "Maybe some other time."

Just then Rex let out a mild roar.

"I better get back down. Rex might think I've abandoned him. Besides, I've also gotta get him settled in his new hiding spot."

"Where's that?"

"Under the boat pond."

"You mean like underwater? Can he breathe underwater? Can he even swim?"

"I don't know. But he can hold his breath for a long time. So even if he can't swim, he can walk along the bottom until he gets to his new hiding place. My Dad has this book about the sewer system. I've been using it to find places for Rex to hide. But he keeps outgrowing the tunnels. There's supposed to be a fairly large cave under the boat pond. It used to be a main sewer line but they closed it off so they wouldn't contaminate the pond."

Davy followed Gretchen as she climbed down from the tree fort. "You really think that's a good place to hide him?" asked Gretchen. "What if some boaters see him?"

"You got a better idea?"

"Well, we know he can climb," said Gretchen as she reached the ground. Davy dropped down behind her.

"Climb? You mean up there?" he said, looking back into the trees.

"Why not?" asked Gretchen. "I saw this program on the Discovery Channel about these twenty-foot-long monitor dragons that live in the trees in New Zealand. Besides, the cave under the boat pond is too risky. Think about it. A couple rent a boat and row across the pond. 'Look dear, isn't that one of those dinosaurs?' 'Why I believe it is. Maybe we should row a little faster.' Get the picture?"

Davy looked back into the tree and then at Rex.

"What do you think, Rex? Think you could live up in the trees for awhile?"

Rex looked up and then turned his head in consideration.

"It's either the trees or the cave under the pond," said Davy.

Undecided, Rex scratched the side of his head with his right claw.

Seeing this, Gretchen just rolled her eyes. "You guys figure it out. I don't like hanging around on the ground too long. Somebody might come along."

"Let's try it in the trees for one night," suggested Davy. "And if that doesn't work, we'll check out the cave under the pond. Besides, Gretchen will be here to keep you company."

Rex looked at Gretchen and seemed to smile.

"Ah, I'm afraid he's gonna have to be up there alone," said Gretchen. "I have to go home in case my mother shows up. But he'll be all right as long as he stays up there. His color blends right in with the leaves."

"Come on, big guy," said Davy. "Just one night. It's gotta be better than that smelly sewer under the subway. One night under the stars."

Rex looked up and then at Davy and Gretchen. He then took reached up and grabbed a branch for support. Using his powerful hind legs, he leaped up to the first branch of the tree. Stopping to look back at Davy and Gretchen, he gave a brief wave goodbye and then moved higher into the tree until he was out of sight.

"I sure hope this works," said Davy.

"I'll come by first thing in the morning and check him out," said Gretchen.

"Thanks," said Davy. "Hey. I'm going to this lecture tomorrow at the Natural History Museum. Would you like to come?"

"That depends. What's it on?"

"Dinosaurs."

"In that case, sure."

"Tomorrow, then. Two o'clock. I'll meet you at the 77th Street entrance. I can get you in for free because my parents work for the museum."

"Cool. Maybe we should bring Rex with us," said Gretchen. "Just kidding. I gotta run. See you tomorrow."

Davy watched as Gretchen ran off into the night. He took one more look up into the high trees but he couldn't see anything.

"Good night, Rex," he said into the tree.

A faint growl came back.

CHAPTER NINE

A long line of people had gathered at the entrance to the museum's auditorium by the time Gretchen arrived. Some of them grumbled when she joined Davy toward the front of the line.

"How was Rex?" asked Davy.

"Sound asleep," said Gretchen. "I decided not to wake him up."

"Good idea."

They entered and took seats in the rear of the auditorium which, being designed like stadium seating, meant they were sitting up high in the back.

The room was full when the lights went down. Only the stage was lit as a curtain parted and Professor Berenson appeared in a black cape. Taking long strides, he walked to a podium as the curtain continued to open further, revealing a large screen behind the stage. On the screen was a drawing of several different types of dinosaurs in various settings.

"Good afternoon, ladies and gentlemen. I am Doctor Jediah Berenson, Chief Paleontologist for the Natural History Museum. I'm also Director of Paleontology at Columbia University."

Davy leaned over and whispered to Gretchen, "He's also a creep." That made Gretchen giggle and some people in the audience "shhhed" her. Davy made an "I'm sorry" face and they turned back toward the stage.

"Today," continued the Professor, "we are going to remove some of the many myths surrounding dinosaurs, talk a bit about how they fit into the evolutionary spectrum, and discuss some of the latest theories about why they became extinct."

As the Professor talked, different slides appeared on the screen behind him.

"First the myths," he said. "In movies, or in books, whenever we see or read about dinosaurs, they are portrayed as large, slow-moving, stupid creatures, smashing everything in their paths. Godzillas."

As he said this, a picture of Godzilla from the movie appeared, and then changed to a photo of several smaller dinosaurs.

"Well, it has come to our knowledge that most dinosaurs were quite a bit smaller than that. In fact, most of them were between five and six feet tall, or, to put it in perspective, about the size of an average human.

"When dinosaurs were first discovered, in the mid-1800s, they were given the name *Dinosaurus*, which means 'terrible lizard.' This perpetuated another myth: that dinosaurs were somehow related to the reptilian family, which means they were cold blooded. In fact, current research indicates dinosaurs were in fact warm blooded and were probably closer to birds and mammals than reptiles."

A slide of the skeletal frame of an ostrich appeared next to that of an *Allosaurus*.

"Dinosaurs ruled the earth for nearly 150 million years. Mankind has been around for only about 100,000 years. Dinosaurs were not slow-moving, dumb creatures. They were swift, and agile, and highly intelligent. They had keen senses and communicated in ways we haven't dreamed of."

A man in the audience raised his hand.

"Excuse me, Professor."

"Yes, sir."

"If dinosaurs were so smart, then why did they become extinct?"

"Possibly for the same reason we may become extinct."

"What does that mean?"

"Well, let me just say that I do not hold with the theory that says a meteor hit the earth and caused the atmosphere to change so dramatically that nothing survived. I believe the dinosaurs experienced something we are facing today: over-consumption. I think the dinosaurs ate their way into extinction by devouring the rain forests, thus destroying the ozone layer that kept out the harmful rays of the sun. A prehistoric version of the kind of global warming we're facing today."

The man in the audience stood staring at the Professor with his mouth open.

"In other words, you think dinosaurs died from the cancer-causing rays of the sun."

Professor Berenson walked out onto the stage in front of a huge dinosaur slide.

"That plus starvation. What if they simply ran out of food and began to devour each other? Or what if they just went underground? The last comment caused a ripple of murmuring throughout the audience.

"A few months ago, I commissioned an expedition to Mount Kilimanjaro in Africa. Since then, we have been analyzing the data sent back from that exhibition, which as you may know, ended in tragedy with the disappearance of Sam and Margaret Ross. Most dinosaur digs have occurred in North America, Montana, and in China. Those digs unearthed some of our best dinosaur fossils, dating back to the early days of the dinosaur. And then we discovered this."

The screen showed a slide of a large skull.

"We were able to determine this was less than ten million years old. It was found in the Sahara Desert. That's when we started looking toward Africa for clues. And it wasn't until the Ross' search for a dinosaur graveyard in a valley on the side of Mount Kilimanjaro that this was found.

"This slide is of a hipbone. This is not a fossil. It's a bone it's only five thousand years old."

Another wave of murmuring floated around the audience.

"You're starting to get my point," said the Professor. "In order to get out of the sun, and the deadly rays, and to find a new source of nourishment we believe some dinosaurs went searching for a place that would protect them."

A woman in the front row raised her hand.

"If what you're saying is true, then is it possible that some dinosaurs could still be alive?"

"A very good possibility, I would say," said Professor Berenson.

This remark caused a noticeable increase in the noise level as audience members conferred with each other.

"Think about it. How else can we account for such sightings of creatures like the Loch Ness Monster? Or the sea creatures they wrote about in the days of Columbus? Anything is possible. More to the point, you can go to the zoo today and see creatures that were around during the time of the dinosuars. They're called alligators. Why should they be the only ones to survive?"

Davy and Gretchen exchanged a glance. "If he only knew," Gretchen whispered.

"That's the problem," said Davy. "I think he does know, or at least he suspects. If he ever found Rex, he'd put him under a microscope and study him to death."

"Have to be a pretty big microscope."

"Or worse. He'd have him stuffed and mounted like all the other animals in the museum."

"We can't let him do that," said Gretchen.

Davy turned toward Gretchen and smiled. It felt good to have an ally. He only wished his Mom and Dad were here. They'd know what to do.

CHAPTER TEN

While Davy and Gretchen listened to the lecture, a young man stood at the 77th Street entrance to Central Park handing out flyers to people walking by. He gave one to a man in a suit who glanced at the flyer and then tossed it into the bushes.

In a tree nearby, Rex was still asleep on a thick branch when a scratching sound caused him to open one eye. He raised his head and looked in the direction of the sound that had awakened him.

On the branch of another tree, a gray squirrel was scraping at a place where a bird had attempted to build a nest.

Rex, who now stood eight feet tall, heard a grumbling sound and looked down at his stomach. That sound could only mean one thing. Rex's stomach was empty and crying out for food. He looked back at the squirrel and was taken by how similar in appearance it was to the animal that had made up the bulk of his most recent diet. To Rex, the squirrel was nothing more than a well-dressed rat.

Estimating the distance between where he lay and the squirrel, Rex prepared to make his move. He inched himself quietly along the branch he was on until the branch began to bend. There was about a four-foot gap between his branch and the one the squirrel was on.

Flexing his strong hind legs, Rex leaped from his branch to the squirrel's branch.

As soon as he landed, the branch began to crack under his weight, even though he landed on the strongest part next to the tree trunk.

The squirrel looked up and saw Rex standing over him. He quickly ran as far down the length of the branch as he could go. Rex tried to follow him but the branch began to bend and then splinter.

Before he could move back up the branch, it snapped off under his feet. Rex tried to reach out and grab another branch to break his fall, but he missed and continued his descent, banging into lower branches and eventually landing in a thick bush that cushioned his fall.

Letting out a deep sigh, Rex started to get up when something else caught his eye.

It was the flyer the man in the business suit had tossed into the bushes. Rex reached over and pulled the flyer up to his face.

He couldn't read what it said, of course, but the picture of a menacing looking *T.rex* surrounded by dozens of other dinosaurs spoke volumes. It was a flyer for the Dinosaurs Alive exhibit on the great lawn of the park just across from the Natural History Museum. Rex snorted at the picture and then ate it.

Meanwhile, Davy and Gretchen had left the lecture and were walking from the museum to the tree where Rex had been sleeping.

"Ya know, in school, I used to think you were kinda dorky," said Gretchen.

"Thanks."

"Well, you were always playing with those stupid wrestling figures. I mean come on. We're almost teenagers."

"You're almost a teenager. I'm still eleven."

"Anyway, I just wanted to say that you're okay, know what I mean? Now that I got to know you."

"You're pretty cool, too."

"I never said you were cool," snapped Gretchen as they reached the tree.

"My mistake," said Davy, as he followed Gretchen up the tree.

"Oh, no!"

"What?" said Davy, pulling himself up to the branch Gretchen was on.

"He's not here," said Gretchen. She then pointed at the tree next to them. "Look."

Davy followed her arm and saw the broken branch of the nearby tree.

"We have to find him," said Davy.

The Dinosaurs Alive exhibit was situated on the great lawn of Central Park with the Natural History Museum in the background. There was a sign at the entrance that read: "Closed—Exhibit Hours are 10 a.m. to 6 p.m." In the rear of the tent, someone or something had torn a hole in the canvas. A distinct grunting sound was coming from the other side.

Next to the tent was a guardhouse with a security guard inside reading a horror comicbook. The uniformed guard heard the grunting sound and looked up. He put down his comic and grabbed a flashlight and looked around the tent.

"Okay," said the guard. "No sneakin' into the exhibit. I'll give you ten seconds and you git. or I call the police."

The guard swept the light around the outside of the tent. He then went inside where the light from the flashlight sent a beam across the large, computerized models of the dinosaurs. The guard looked around and shook his head. Unable to see anything out of place, he left the tent and headed back to his guard shack.

As soon as the guard left the tent, one of the dinosaurs scratched its head.

It was near sundown when Davy bowed his head in defeat. They had searched the entire length of Gretchen's elaborate tree fortress when they determined Rex was no longer there.

Now they were in the bushes under the broken branch. They could see an outline of where Rex had fallen.

"I lost him," said Davy.

"He'll turn up," said Gretchen.

"That's what I'm afraid of," said Davy. "It's getting dark and I have to get home or my grandmother will start to worry about me."

"You go on," said Gretchen. "I'll keep searching. Nobody knows this park better than I do. Besides, if somebody did find him, it will be on television."

"I just hate to leave him out here like this."

"I think he can take care of himself," said Gretchen. "Go home."

Davy hesitated and then started to leave when Gretchen stepped close to him and kissed him on the cheek.

"We'll find him," she said. "Now get going. There's nothing more we can do tonight. And if you stay out any later, your grandmother will call the police."

"What about you? Won't your mother be worried, too?"

"Well, you see, that would only happen if she was home. But how likely is that? I'll be okay. You get going."

Davy didn't like leaving Gretchen in the park alone, but she was right. If he didn't get back to the apartment soon, he'd be grounded.

Davy let himself into the apartment quietly, hoping to avoid detection, but his grandmother was already waiting in the hallway.

"Davy! Where have you been?"

"I'm sorry, Grandma. I met a friend and we forgot about the time."

"You should have called. I was worried sick. A boy your age, out this late."

"I'm not a baby anymore, Grandma."

"You're still too young to be running around this city at night. And your supper's all cold. I don't know what I'm gonna do with you."

"I'm sorry, Grandma. You're right. I should have called."

"I can reheat your supper."

"I'm not very hungry."

"You're not? That's a first."

"I am tired. I think I'll go to bed early."

Davy started to head for his bedroom when his Grandma stood in front of him.

"Davy," said Grandma Becky. "There's somebody here to see you."

As soon as she said it, Professor Berenson stepped into the hallway from the living room, holding a cup of coffee.

"Hello, Davy."

"Professor Berenson."

"What did you think of my lecture?"

"How did you know I was there?"

"You were sitting in the top row, with a young lady I believe. Did what I say make sense to you?"

"I don't know what you mean."

"I think you do, Davy. I think you know very well." The Professor knelt down on one knee so he could be eye level with Davy. "Did you know that you're the spitting image of your mother?"

"My mother? I always thought I looked like my father."

"Yes. There's a slight resemblance there as well."

"Can I get you some more coffee, Professor?" asked Grandma Becky.

"I'm fine, thank you. If you don't mind, I'd like to talk to Davy in private somewhere. Is that okay?"

Grandma Becky considered the request with a pensive look. "I suppose so. I'll just be in the kitchen if you need me," she said, leaving the hallway.

Davy eyed the Professor with caution.

"Why don't we sit in the living room?"

Davy followed him into the room and took a seat on the sofa. The Professor stood by the fireplace.

"Why is it I have the feeling that what I said today was 'old hat' to you?" said the Professor.

"Old hat? What are you talking about?"

"Are you missing something, Davy?"

The question sent a shiver down Davy's spine. "Missing? What?"

"This," said the Professor, as he reached into his pocket pulled out the egg.

Davy looked at it wide-eyed as the Professor rested the empty eggshell on the coffee table in front of the sofa. Davy let out a deep sigh of relief. He thought he was talking about Rex. It was just the egg Rex came out of. How did the Professor get it?

"When I first came into possession of the egg, I assumed it was like the other bone samples discovered by your parents. It wasn't until later that I decided to do my own age analysis. You were there, weren't you?"

"Where?"

"When it hatched."

"Professor, I still don't know what you're talking about."

"Okay. It doesn't matter. One day, I will want to know what happened. But for now, all I want you to know is that I know. And that I'll be watching. I must tell you that we don't have all that much time."

"What are you talking about?"

"Another expedition to Mount Kilimanjaro."

"That's where my parents were when that earthquake happened," Davy said excitedly. "Are you going to try to find them?"

"No. I'm afraid not. We've already searched everywhere. It's been months. Any chance of survival are slim to none."

"Don't say that," said Davy, disappointed and slumping back onto the sofa.

"I know it's hard for you to believe it, Davy. Especially without seeing their bodies. The lack of closure. It makes it that much harder to let go."

"But I don't want to let go."

"Good. Then perhaps you'll help me."

"Help you. How?"

"I think you know," said the Professor, moving closer and pinning Davy to the sofa. "If by some miracle your parents are alive, the longer we wait to find them, the less chance they'll have to survive. Do the right thing, Davy. It's all up to you now."

"Why is it up to me?"

"Because you have the key. Expeditions cost money. The museum isn't going to pay for another one. But you have something that could help us get the necessary funding without any trouble."

"When are you going?"

"That depends on you."

The Professor picked up the egg and put it back in his pocket.

"You can either cooperate with us, or not. Think about it. Just remember that time is of the essence. Your parents' lives, if they are alive, could be in your hands. Why don't you sleep on it? We can talk in the morning."

The Professor started to walk toward the front door when he whirled around.

"There can only be one master species, Davy. Man and dinosaur could never co-exist."

"You're wrong."

The Professor's eyes widened and he smiled.

Ooops, thought Davy.

"I knew it."

Davy realized he had given away the secret.

"I mean. You must be wrong."

"I'm a scientist. Prove me wrong, Davy. Show me."

The Professor walked out the door.

Davy couldn't sleep well that night. He kept waking up out of a dream, a nightmare, where he and Rex were at sea on a ship in a storm and the boat was going to sink when a rescue boat showed up. The only the person on the rescue boat was the Professor.

CHAPTER ELEVEN

Parents and children gathered outside the Dinosaurs Alive exhibit tent waiting for the door to open. Inside, the manager of the exhibit, Tom McDermott, a 35-year-old former amusement park ride manager, checked the equipment, making sure everything was operational. His round-faced younger assistant, Gregg Moon, inspected the switches and connections.

"Are we ready, Mr. Moon?"

"Just about," said Gregg, who was a chunky 20-year-old NYU student trying to make a few extra bucks between classes.

"What's holding us up?"

"Someone broke into the candy machines and ate all the candy," said Gregg. "I'm just waiting to hear they've been restocked. Meanwhile, I'm plugging our dinosaurs in. We left them unplugged overnight."

"Forget about waiting for the candy. Just get these babies operable before a mob forms outside," ordered Tom.

"If you say so. Just one more to go."

Gregg knelt down behind a *Triceratops* and plugged something into a socket.

"Okay. Start em' up," said Gregg.

Tom threw a switch and the lights came on, revealing a room full of huge creatures that looked so life-like. A *Triceratops* began to battle with a *Stegosaurus*. *Pterodactyl*s began flying over head. The large *Tyrannosaurus* began to growl. The not-so-large *T.rex* started to look around, somewhat confused and bewildered. It was Rex and he was definitely confused as he tried to communicate with his fellow dinosaurs who continued to ignore him.

Tom the manager gave the exhibit a quick scan with his eyes and then went to the cash register and opened his booth.

"It's show time."

Gregg opened the front door and the line of people began to move forward and inside.

A few blocks away on Central Park West, Davy ate a bowl of cereal while Grandma Becky read the morning newspaper. Davy wasn't paying attention at first as he devoured the Cap'n Crunch, but then he looked up and saw the back page of the paper his grandmother was reading. Suddenly he knew where Rex might be.

There was a full-page ad for the Dinosaurs Alive exhibit.

"It says here the police are warning people about staying in the park after dark," said Grandma Becky from behind the paper. "But it doesn't say why. Isn't that strange?"

She continued reading, holding the paper open. When she realized she did not get a response to her question, she lowered the paper and saw that Davy was no longer sitting in his seat.

"Where'd he go now?" she asked.

In the background, she could hear the front door open and close.

"Davy? Did you hear what I said? Don't go in the park."

Back at the Dinosaurs Alive exhibit, a little boy stared up at Rex, who seemed to be trying to mimic the movements of the computerized fake dinosaurs. The large T.rex growled and turned its head, trying to look mean. Rex watched for a few seconds, then he tried to growl, too, but it came out sounding like someone clearing his throat, sort of guttural and not intimidating.

The little boy, whose name was Timothy, started to laugh.

Rex smiled down at Timothy. Then Rex laughed his own form of laughter, which made Timothy stand straight and take notice.

"Wow," said Timothy, astonished that one of the dinosaurs had actually responded to him.

While Rex and Timothy were trading laughs, Davy came out the door of his brownstone and ran off down the street. Across the street, and from out behind a tree, stepped Professor Berenson. He smiled to himself and started to follow Davy.

Back inside the Dinosaurs Alive exhibit tent, Timothy was tugging on his mother's skirt.

"Mom."

"What, honey?"

"That dinosaur laughed at me," said Timothy.

"Isn't that nice," said his mother. "They look so real. Where's your sister?"

It was then the sound of a little girl crying spread through the tent.

"Sarah's crying," said Timothy.

After following the sound of crying, Timothy and his mother found Sarah at the far end of the exhibit. The three-year-old girl was sobbing and pointing up at a mean-looking *Pterodactyl* hanging by a thin wire, circling overhead, looking for prey.

"Don't cry, Sarah," said her mother. "It's not real."

"Sarah's scared of the big bird," said Timothy. "Maybe my new friend can help."

"Friend?" asked his mother.

Timothy walked back over to where Rex had positioned himself.

"Hey!" called Timothy.

Rex looked down at the boy and turned his head to the side.

Timothy pointed back toward the flying *Pterodactyl* and said, "That big ugly thing is scaring my sister."

Rex looked up at the winged dinosaur and thought about it. He then nodded and followed Timothy as he returned to his Mom and sister, who were looking up at the *Pterodactyl*.

"Watch this," Timothy said.

They all looked on as Rex climbed up on a fake rock and waited for the *Pterodactyl* to swing by. When it did, Rex reached out and snapped off its head, causing the entire contraption to fall to the floor in a loud crash!

Timothy's Mom had her mouth wide open in disbelief. Timothy was smiling proudly. His sister was staring bug-eyed.

At the front desk, Tom and Gregg heard the crash and looked at each other.

"I'll check it out," said Gregg.

Rex had climbed back down from the rock and had resumed his position by the time Gregg showed up to find Timothy's Mom scolding her son.

Timothy's sister was staring at the floor where Gregg found the headless Pterodactyl. Gregg knelt down to inspect the damage as a crowd formed around the mess of wires and cables and the headless dinosaur on the floor.

Gregg looked up and saw dozens of eyes staring at him.

"Okay, everybody back," he ordered as he stood up. "Did anyone see what happened?"

Timothy's Mom took Timothy by his arm and dragged him over to Gregg.

"I'm really sorry," she said. "I don't even know how he did it."

Gregg glared down at Timothy.

"Didn't you see the signs? You're not supposed to touch the dinosaurs, son."

Timothy pulled his arm away from his mother.

"I didn't touch your silly fake dinosaurs."

"You're not supposed to throw anything at them, either. This *Pterodactyl* cost several thousand dollars."

"I didn't do anything."

"Then how did it happen?"

"He did it," said Timothy, pointing over to where Rex had been standing. But Rex was no longer there.

"What? The *Tyrannosaurus* rex? How?"

"Not him. The little one," insisted Timothy.

"What little one?" asked Gregg.

Timothy looked all around.

"He's gone."

Gregg gave Timothy a suspicious look. He turned to Timothy's mother and said, "Okay, look. I think I can repair this thing. But it might be better if you and your children left the exhibit."

"Yes. Of course," she said, relieved she would not have to pay for a broken thousand-dollar fake dinosaur. "I'm sure it was an accident. He didn't mean to break anything. He must have hit a control or something."

Gregg nodded and escorted Timothy, his Mom and sister out of the exhibit.

Meanwhile, back in the rear of the tent, behind some fake scenery, Rex poked his head out to see if the commotion he caused had died down. It appeared as if everything were back to normal, so he stepped out of the plastic bushes and began walking across a papier mâché swamp. He was about halfway across when a *Triceratops* on rollers slid over and poked Rex's tail with its horn.

Rex stopped, turned around, and grabbed the *Triceratops* by one of its three horns. He pushed up until the electrical cord connected to a control box snapped and sent sparks flying as the huge beast toppled over on its side.

He was about to continue when a smattering of applause caused Rex to stop and turn toward a small crowd of people, adults and children, clapping their hands in appreciation of an awesome performance. Rex bowed to the ovation.

"That was great," said a father to his little girl.

"This show just gets better and better," said another parent.

Rex took another bow and when he came up he saw over the heads of the audience to the far end of the exhibit. Gregg was rushing toward him.

"Hey!" yelled Gregg.

A little boy standing in the small crowded tugged at his father's hand until the father looked down.

"Daddy. Look. That dinosaur isn't plugged in like all the others."

The boy's father looked down at Rex's feet as Rex continued to move across the swamp. And sure enough, the boy was right. The father thought for a moment and then smiled to himself.

"Must be some kind of remote control. Ya know with computers and things, you can do a lot of stuff you couldn't do before."

Rex continued on and disappeared just as Gregg arrived to find *Triceratops* on its side.

"Not again," said Gregg.

A man in the audience tapped Gregg on the shoulder.

"Great touch," said the man. "Good show. Do you lease this out for corporate parties?"

"Huh?" said Gregg, staring down at the *Triceratops* and at the snapped cable. He quickly looked around at the crowd. Did that kid sneak back in? But how could he, when he was with Gregg being escorted out the front door? There must be another vandal lurking about. And Gregg was determined to find him. He looked at the fake bushes and anywhere else someone could be hiding.

"Okay. Come on out," said Gregg as he entered the swamp. "I know you're in here."

There was still a long line of people waiting to get into the Dinosaurs Alive exhibit when Davy arrived. He knew it was wrong to cut in line, but he didn't have time to wait. Besides, he wasn't interested in the exhibit, which he'd seen about a million times. He had a more important mission, to find Rex before the Professor or someone else did.

So he went to the front of the line and told the family waiting to buy a ticket that his family was already inside and would they mind if he went in ahead of them.

While they debated this among themselves, Davy watched the people coming out and listened to what they said.

"That one dinosaur was so life-like," said a woman to her two boys who kept punching each other as she struggled to get them out of the way.

Another woman following her said, "My four-year-old wet his pants, he was so scared. They should warn you about that. It's too frightening for little children, especially when that one dinosaur ripped the head off that giant bird."

Hmm, thought Davy. That doesn't sound like the show he'd seen.

An older man and woman were leaving and the old man looked distressed.

"I thought I was gonna have a heart attack when that thing turned that other dinosaur over."

I'd better get in there *fast*, Davy told himself. While the man and woman argued over whether to let Davy go ahead of them, Davy waited until a large group was leaving, and then slipped in around them so the person taking tickets couldn't see him.

As soon as he was inside, someone in a long dark coat joined the line outside. The Professor didn't see Davy when he arrived to take his place at the end of the line. He looked up at the large poster of the exhibit and smiled.

Inside the tent, Davy immediately began his search for Rex. He saw Gregg and Tom in the rear of the exhibit in the swamp. They were pushing the *Triceratops* to its upright position.

"You've been busy, haven't you, Rex?" said Davy aloud.

Nearby, Rex was slurping water from a fake prehistoric stream. He looked up when he heard his name.

At the line outside, the Professor finally made it to the ticket booth, paid one adult fare, and entered the tent. Inside he gazed around at the lifelike creatures. He smiled widely at the inaccurate depictions. Still, he figured if a dinosaur was running around New York City, this was as likely a place as any for it to stop. After all, it would feel right at home here, even if they got it all wrong. The Professor scanned the exhibit and the dozen or so scenarios. A perplexed expression washed over his face. "That's ridiculous," he said, and walked toward a group of dinosaurs next to a sign that said "Brontosaurus."

"They obviously haven't kept up with the literature," snapped the Professor as he took down the sign. He then took out a magic marker and put a thick line through the name "Brontosaurus" and then wrote "*Apatosaurus*" over it.

"That's better," he said.

Meanwhile, in another part of the exhibit, Davy was searching for signs of Rex, when something nudged him from behind. "Hey," he exclaimed, and then turned to find Rex standing behind him with a wide, toothy grin.

"Rex," said Davy, throwing his arms him, "you've been a naughty boy."

Rex smiled shyly and turned his head to the side.

"How am I gonna get you out of here without being seen?"

Rex shook his head "no."

"Well, we can't stay here."

Rex moved his head "no" again and then looked all around at the other dinosaurs.

"I get it. You want to take them with us."

Rex nodded "yes."

"They're not real."

Rex looked confused.

"Look," said Davy as he picked up an electrical cord leading from the wall to a Stegasaurus. The steggy was moving its head back and forth, until Davy pulled the cord out of the wall and it stopped moving.

"See? I unplugged it and now it can't move."

Back at the newly titled *Apatosaurus* exhibit, Professor Berenson was staring up at the huge beast, shaking his head.

"That's not how they did it," said the Professor.

Professor Berenson looked around the exhibit to see if anyone was watching. Then he climbed into the exhibit and removed a fake leaf from the mouth of a baby *Apatosaurus*. He began to tear up the leaf.

"This is the way it should look," he said, grinding the leaf into tiny pieces.

Just then Gregg looked over and saw the Professor.

"There's the culprit," he said, and ran toward the exhibit.

The Professor had the leaf in just the right pulpy state when he looked up and saw Gregg glaring at him.

"Do you work here, young man?" asked the Professor.

"What do you think you're doing?" replied Gregg, as he stared at the mushy leaf in the Professor's hand.

"Correcting a number of obvious mistakes," said the Professor. "First, this is not a Brontosaurus. It's an *Apatosaurus*. There is no such thing as a Brontosaurus. It was actually a composite of several different dinosaurs. But mostly it was an *Apatosaurus* so I've fixed your sign. Second, a baby *Apatosaurus* is born without teeth. So the parents chew the food first and then deposit the chewed food into the baby's mouth. You would never see a full leaf in a baby *Apatosaurus'* mouth."

"No kidding. Now, would you please get out of the exhibit? We don't need any more accidents today."

"Oh. Have you been having some problems?"

Davy was trying to figure out how he was going to get Rex out of the tent without anyone seeing them when he spotted some canvas.

"Come on," said Davy. "I've got an idea."

But as Davy headed for the canvas, Rex noticed a control panel and smiled. He reached out and touched some of the buttons. This caused the lights to flicker on and off.

Davy stopped, turned back, and grabbed Rex by the hand. He then led him toward the canvas.

Gregg was about to say something else when the lights flickered.

"Now what?" said Gregg.

The Professor looked out among the crowd. In the back of the tent and about four scenarios away, he saw Davy leading a rather tall object, apparently under a sheet of canvas. The Professor started to follow Davy when he felt a hand on his arm and looked back. The hand belonged to Gregg.

"Where do you think you're going?" asked Gregg.

"Would you please take your hand off my arm?" said the Professor.

"Something funny is going on around here, and I think you know what it is."

"Yes. Well, what would you say if I told you there was a real dinosaur loose among your exhibits?"

"I'd say you were nuts."

"I thought so." And with that, the Professor stuck a hypodermic needle into Gregg's hand, which was still holding the Professor's arm.

"Ouch! Hey."

But before he could say another word, Gregg closed his eyes and slumped to the floor.

"Sweet dreams, my friend. I wonder what dinosaurs dream about? Let's find out."

Professor Berenson checked his needle and saw there was plenty of liquid still inside. He put the needle away and walked off into the crowd in the direction he'd seen Davy go, leaving Gregg snoring in the *Apatosaurus* exhibit.

Davy was leading Rex toward the rear exit when the canvas covering Rex snagged on a nail and it pulled off. Davy looked back and saw Rex was without the canvas. "Ooops," said Davy.

Across the aisle, a small boy of about five saw Davy leading Rex toward the exit.

"Hey!" cried the boy. "That kid just stole one of the dinosaurs."

Tom, the exhibit manager, looked up from his calculator when he heard the remark.

"What? Somebody's what?" he barked, standing up. "Where's Gregg?"

Tom ran over to the boy. "What did you say, son?"

"I just saw somebody leave 'with one of the dinosaurs."

"You did? Where?"

The boy pointed to an exit. "Right over there," he said.

In the rear of the exhibit, Professor Berenson moved slowly through the crowd that had gathered around the recently up-righted *Triceratops*. He was studying the faces of the children when he saw Davy behind an older couple and their two grandchildren. Davy moved sideways toward the rear exit and the canvas was moving along next to him. The Professor reached into his pocket and pulled out his needle. He then slowly slithered through the crowd like a snake in tall grass, holding the needle to his side so he wouldn't accidentally stick someone.

As he got closer to the rear of the exhibit tent, he could see the canvas up ahead. It had stopped moving. Now was the time to strike. The Professor squeezed between a woman and her daughter and slid up behind the canvas. Then, carefully, without arousing too much attention, he pressed the needle through the canvas fabric until it penetrated whatever was underneath.

Smiling to himself, he plunged the needle as deep as it would go and then pressed down on the plunger.

"Sweet dreams," he whispered, as he pulled the needle away and put it back in his pocket. Then, he reached out and grabbed a fist full of canvas and pulled it away.

As the canvas dropped to the floor of the tent, several people turned and gasped. The *Tyrannosaurus rex* roared at them and they moved back. The Professor pulled out the needle and gave the beast another shot.

"You're a lot stronger than I expected," he said. Then he noticed something on the floor next to the dinosaur. It was an electrical cord, and it was connected to the *T.rex*.

"What?" exclaimed the Professor as he knelt down to examine his discovery.

"Don't tell me," snapped the Professor. "I just drugged a fake dinosaur. Davy! Davy! I know you're in here."

He removed his needle from the lifelike skin of the animatronic dinosaur and was about to look for Davy when he realized Tom, the exhibit's manager, was staring at him.

"What do you think you're doing?"

"Well, ah," the Professor stammered. Even he couldn't come up with a quick explanation.

"Are you the one who's trying to steal one of my dinosaurs?"

"What?" replied the Professor.

"I just got word somebody's trying to steal a dinosaur," said Tom, in a louder than necessary voice.

The Professor was about to speak when he looked across the tent and saw Davy near the front door.

"He's getting away!" yelled the Professor as he tried to run after Davy, but Tom grabbed him from behind and held him back.

"Guard!" screamed Tom.

Davy looked back and saw the Professor and Tom struggling.

"Just hold on there, pal," ordered Tom.

The last thing Davy saw before he and Rex slipped out of the tent was the Professor reaching into the pocket of his black coat.

As soon as they got outside, Davy pushed Rex into the bushes and out of sight.

"The Professor is in there, Rex. He must have followed me. We have to get away from here, fast."

Rex looked at Davy with an expression of thought on his face, which was quite an accomplishment for a dinosaur since his facial muscles weren't that developed. Still, the expression on Rex's face definitely indicated that an idea had formed. What that idea was, Davy had no clue. Nor did Rex have anyway of telling him.

"What?" asked Davy. Rex considered the question and answered by walking off.

"Hey. Where are you going?"

Davy followed Rex through the bushes. As they moved deeper into the park, Rex kept looking up into the trees. Davy watched him for a while and then his eyes widened.

"I get it. You want to go to Gretchen's tree house."

Rex turned and nodded.

Inside the Dinosaurs Alive tent, the security guard arrived to find Tom lying on the floor of the tent, snoring and using a foot of the *Tyrannosaurus* as a pillow. The guard scanned the crowd of people standing over Tom and staring at him.

"What happened here?" asked the guard.

"He was talking to some man in a black cape, and then he just fell down and went to sleep," said a little girl holding on to her grandfather's hand.

After searching everywhere inside the tent, the Professor decided Davy must have gotten out. He found a rear exit flap, stuck his head out and looked around. "Where did they go?" he wondered. Then he saw some movement in the bushes heading toward the park.

"Ah-hah," he exclaimed, and headed in that direction. As he followed the movement, the Professor pulled out his needle and attached a new bottle of fluid. That done, he continued following the movement deeper into the park. He had walked about another hundred yards and realized he was standing in a grove of trees. He also realized the movement had stopped. He parted the bushes, but there was nothing behind them except some old rusted soda cans and gum wrappers.

With a clenched fist, he punched the air. "I lost them," he snarled, and reached into his pocket. This time, instead of pulling out a needle, he pulled out a cellular phone. He punched in some numbers and spoke.

"Hello. Jackson. It's me. I almost had him. I'm in the park. Get 20 of your best men. I want every inch of this park covered. I know it's in here somewhere. I mean, where else could you hide an eight-foot dinosaur?"

CHAPTER TWELVE

High above the Professor, in a tall tree just over his head, two children and a dinosaur listened to his cell phone conversation.

"We've got about four more hours of sunlight, so hurry," said the Professsor. "I'll meet you at the West 77th Street entrance. We'll start the search there. Bring dogs. They can track its scent. Just in case. Bring a chainsaw."

Davy looked at Gretchen with panic in his eyes.

"Dogs? Chainsaw?" he whispered. "We're dead."

Gretchen looked down through the branches and saw the Professor fold up his phone and put it away.

"We have to leave the park," said Davy.

"Why? Even with dogs, they'll never find you up here."

"How can you be so sure?"

"I've been up here for three years now and nobody's found me yet."

"Was anyone really looking? This Professor is crazy. He's not gonna stop until he gets Rex."

"I don't know what else to tell you," said Gretchen.

Suddenly, Rex stepped on a branch that wasn't quite big enough to support his ever-increasing weight. The branch snapped like a twig and the sound was like a gunshot echoing through the treetops.

The sound startled the Professor, who immediately looked up at the trees.

"What was that?" he asked himself as he tried to see through the thick leaves and branches. Something was up there. But what was it? Actually, something was falling down toward him, and he'd better move out of the—

Crash!

"Aggghhh!" screamed the Professor.

The broken branch landed with a crashing thud about two inches from the Professor, who was frozen and afraid to move. He opened his eyes and saw that he was covered with dead leaves and pieces of bark. Shaking his head and coming to his senses, he began to slowly walk away from the trees and toward the bushes leading to the 77th Street entrance.

As he walked away, he stole glances up into the trees, wondering if the falling branch was a simple act of nature, or if someone had sent it hurling at him on purpose.

This was a question best answered when his forces arrived. He looked at his watch as he walked away from the fallen branch. In ten more minutes, things would be different.

Davy let out a sigh of relief as he watched the Professor walk away from the tree. Rex nudged his side and he petted the dinosaur's head. "He's gone for now," said Davy.

Rex responded by licking Davy's hand as if he was a friendly puppy.

"Yuck," said Gretchen, who made a face at the slime Rex left on the back of Davy's hand.

Davy looked at the foamy spittle and wiped it off on his jeans. "You get used to it after awhile," he said. "Maybe if the Professor could just see how friendly he is."

"Yeah. Maybe they'll put him in a petting zoo. Let the little kiddies feed the dinosaur. Get slimed by a T.rex."

"If only my parents were here," said Davy. "They'd know what to do."

"Seems to me it was your parents who got you into this mess."

"What does that mean?" said Davy.

"Didn't they send you the egg? No note. No instructions. What do they do? They disappear. Hey, as far as I'm concerned, that's what parents do. As soon as you really need them, they disappear."

Davy looked at Gretchen and saw the sadness in her eyes.

The Professor stood at the 77th Street entrance to Central Park and watched a black van arrive. The rear doors opened and Jackson, followed by a dozen other men and four bloodhounds, jumped out of the back of the van. The Professor reached into his pocket and pulled out the eggshell. The dogs sniffed the egg and immediately began to bark. Then, all four of them raced off into the park.

"Whatever was in that thing must be close. They picked up the scent as soon as they smelled it," said Jackson.

The Professor watched with amazement as the dogs disappeared into the park. The hunters ran after them. A wide smile formed on the Professor's face. He had the feeling that this was going to be it. Could he really be this close to the greatest discovery ever?

Rex heard them first but he didn't know what they were. Then Davy heard the sound of dogs barking. The sound was getting louder, which could only mean one thing. They were getting closer.

"Oh, no," said Davy. "Dogs!"

The dogs were running full speed and barking. The Professor, Jackson and the hunters had to sprint to keep up with them.

"They've definitely picked up the scent," said Jackson, gasping for breath.

Gretchen, Davy, and Rex moved higher into the trees. Down below, the sound of barking was getting louder.

"We're trapped," said Davy.

"Maybe not. If we get high enough, maybe the breeze will blow away the scent," said Gretchen.

"I don't think Rex can climb much higher."

In fact, Rex was having trouble reaching the next branch. When he did, the branch snapped and Rex started to fall but caught himself.

The dogs circled a large tree and were barking and jumping around the trunk when the Professor and the hunters arrived.

The Professor looked up into the tree, but there were so many branches and leaves, he couldn't see anything. He turned to Jackson.

"I need that piece of equipment I asked you to bring."

"The chainsaw?" asked Jackson.

"I hope you brought a big one."

Jackson looked at the tree and nodded. "Big enough."

Davy and Gretchen struggled to pull Rex up to a sturdy branch.

"This is about as far as we can go," said Gretchen. "The higher branches won't hold him."

Davy looked at Rex and saw that he was shaking. Rex was looking everywhere but down. "I don't think Rex likes heights." He turned toward Gretchen and said, "I'm sorry I got you into this."

"Why?"

"They're gonna find out about your hiding place."

"That's okay. I was getting a little bored here. I was gonna try rooftops next."

"I'm taking him down," said Davy. "He's scared to death up here and I don't want them to find this place. Even if you leave, someone else might be able to use it." Davy started to climb down when Gretchen reached out.

"No!" she said.

"It's over, Gretchen. He's got us. Why should you have to suffer?"

"He doesn't have you yet."

They heard the sound of the chainsaw start up in an ugly buzz.

"That does it. Thanks, Gretchen," said Davy. "Come on, Rex."

Rex was eager to get out of the tree.

"Please don't go down there," begged Gretchen.

"He's gonna cut down your tree."

"I don't care."

"Well, I care. Come on, Rex. At least we can save the tree."

Davy and Rex began their descent. Reluctantly, Gretchen started to follow them down when one of the hunters moved toward the tree with the chainsaw. The saw was running at full speed.

"The rest of you men better stand back there," said the Professor, pointing to a safe distance from where the tree might fall.

The hunter pulled a pair of safety goggles down over his eyes and slanted the chainsaw toward the bark of the tall old tree. The saw was less than an inch from cutting into wood when a man's voice called out, "Stop!"

The hunter pulled back the saw and turned around.

"You there! Put down that saw!" ordered a man wearing a park services uniform. He was with somebody else and as they got closer, the Professor recognized who the other man was. It was Tom, the manager of Dinosaurs Alive. And he was with two uniformed police officers. Tom saw the Professor and pointed to him.

"That's the man who drugged me!" cried Tom.

"Put down that saw, sir," said the park services officer as he approached the hunter, who turned off the chainsaw and put it on the ground. As soon as he did, he and the other hunters ran off in different directions, leaving Jackson and the Professor to deal with the police.

The Professor watched his men run off and shook his head. He then turned to the two police officers.

"Officers, I'm Dr. Jediah Berenson, Chief Paleontologist with the Natural History Museum."

"I'm Officer Dicker and this is Officer Daniels," said the policeman. "I'm afraid I'm going to have to place you under arrest."

"That won't be necessary, officer," said the Professor, "if you'll let me explain this misunderstanding."

"You are being charged with felonious assault of this gentleman here," said Officer Dicker, nodding at Tom as he said it. "Not to mention a violation of the city's leash laws, and what appears to be an attempt to destroy government property by cutting down one our city's finer trees."

The officer took out a card and read the Miranda statement, which police are required to do if they charge someone in an arrest. "Any statements you make now may be used in a court of law. If you wish to remain silent until you have a lawyer present, that is your right. If you can't afford one, one will be appointed."

"What would you say if I told you there was a dinosaur in this tree?" asked the Professor.

Officer Dicker looked at Tom.

"There was a report that someone was stealing a dinosaur but when we checked, none of them was missing," said Tom.

"I'm not talking about one of those fake dinosaurs," said the Professor, his eyes gleaming. "I'm talking about a *real* dinosaur. A real live *Tyrannosaurus rex*."

"I see," said Officer Dicker. "Why don't you come with me, now? We can take your entire statement downtown."

"You don't believe me."

"Sure I do," said Dicker, obviously trying to humor what he believed to be a very disturbed person. "It's just that right now, we have some other business to attend to. So, if you don't mind, please come with us."

The Professor tried to make a run for it, but the officers restrained him.

"Better get the straight jacket for this one," said Dicker to his partner. "He's seeing real dinosaurs in the trees."

From their concealed spot high up in the tree, Davy, Rex, and Gretchen watched the police escort the Professor and Jackson away in handcuffs.

"That was too close," said Davy.

"We can't stay here anymore, that's for sure. As soon as the Professor gets out of jail he'll be back here before you can say Jurassic Park."

"This might be the only chance I have," said Davy.

"Chance for what?" asked Gretchen.

"To get into the Professor's office while he's not there."

"Why do you want to do that?"

"Come with me and I'll show you."

"I'll come with you but you have to tell me first," insisted Gretchen as she climbed down out of the tree.

When they reached the ground, Rex hugged the tree and then rolled on the ground.

"Somebody's real happy to be back on the ground," said Davy.

"So, are you gonna tell me?" asked Gretchen.

"The Professor said he's planning another trip to the place where my parents disappeared. It's on this mountain in Africa. I bet he has a map somewhere in his office that would show exactly where they were last seen."

"Even if he does, what good is that going to do you?" asked Gretchen.

"I don't know," admitted Davy. "But maybe if I can get into the Professor's office, I'll figure something out."

"We just can't walk into the Natural History Museum with him," said Gretchen, nodding toward Rex, who was doing summersaults.

"You're right," said Davy as he began to think about how to solve this little dilemma. That was when it hit him.

"Wait. Do you realize what tonight is?"

"Ah, Thursday?"

"It's Halloween," said Davy. "Rex, how would you like to go trick or treating?"

Rex smiled and nodded.

"You don't even know what Halloween is," said Davy.

Rex nodded "yes."

"He must sense it's something that would be good to do," said Gretchen. "Remember what the Professor said at the lecture? Dinosaurs have highly developed methods of communication. He might not be able to read words, but he can read you, and if you want to do it, Rex trusts that it's something he wants to do. What I don't understand is how will Halloween get us into the museum and the Professor's office?"

CHAPTER THIRTEEN

Twilight time came to the Big Apple. The sun set over the Hudson River. Dark clouds formed in the sky over the upper West Side as streetlights clicked on. Small groups of children dressed in costumes and holding trick or treat bags patrolled the streets like armies of tiny soldiers. They moved from apartment building to apartment building along Central Park West, where jack o' lanterns sparkled in several windows along the way. A chilly October wind blew down the side streets, kicking up wind funnels of leaves and papers.

Grandma Becky set out a bowl of candy in the living room when the doorbell buzzed. She carried the bowl to the front door and opened it. A group of children in various costumes stood on the stoop of the brownstone.

"Trick or treat," they said in unison.

"Okay, but just take one," she said as she held the bowl out to the children. After they grabbed their candy, they scattered off down the steps of the brownstone. Behind them stood a young boy dressed in a business suit and wearing a mask. He was with his mother and he seemed afraid to approach Grandma Becky. So she knelt down so the boy could see into the bowl.

"Just don't give me any broccoli," he said. "I hate broccoli."

"Broccoli? Who gives out broccoli on Halloween?" asked Grandma Becky.

"You'd be surprised what people give out," said the mother. "We've gotten potatoes, broccoli, tofu. Tofu is the worst because it gets all over everything in the bag."

"Well, no tofu here, just candy," said Grandma Becky. "I like your mask. Who is it? Alfred E. Newman?"

"He's supposed to be George W. Bush," said the boy's mother.

"I see. I thought it was George W.'s father who hated the broccoli," said Grandma Becky as they left.

She shut the door and was putting the bowl down when Davy, dressed as Robin Hood, and Gretchen, made up as Maid Marion, entered the living room, followed by a nearly nine-foot tall "Big Bird."

"Look at you kids," said Grandma Becky. "I want you back by ten o'clock, now."

"Sure thing, Grandma."

"You all look so adorable," said Grandma Becky. "I'm so happy you made such nice friends."

She opened the door as Davy, Gretchen and Rex in disguise left the brownstone. Rex didn't quite fit through the door, so he bent down and tried to push through, but he was stuck on both sides.

"Let me help," said Grandma Becky, giving Rex a shove as he squeezed through the front door.

"Kids are sure growing bigger these days," she added, closing the door behind them.

It took Davy, Rex, and Gretchen about ten minutes to walk from Davy's brownstone to the Natural History Museum. But when they got there, it was dark.

"Now what do we do?" said Gretchen.

"There must be a way in," said Davy.

They walked around to the 77th Street entrance and found a guard who was reading a horror novel in the guard station next to the entrance to the museum. He looked up and saw Davy, Gretchen and Rex as "Big Bird" standing in front of him.

"The museum's closed," he said.

"We know that. We're trick or treating," said Davy.

"Trick or treating, huh. I ain't got any treats, so beat it."

"That's not how it works," said Gretchen.

"How what works?"

"Trick or treat."

"Oh yeah? I suppose you're gonna play some trick on me now. Okay, go on. Let's see it."

Gretchen nodded to Rex, who nodded to her. The guard rolled his eyes.

Then Rex reached out and picked the guard up and turned him upside down until a big key ring fell out.

"Hey! Put me down!" shouted the guard.

Gretchen grabbed the key ring and tossed it to Davy, who ran to the entrance of the museum. As Davy tried each key until he found the right one, Rex lowered the guard to the floor.

"Just who do you think you are?" asked the guard, as he tried to stand up.

Rex considered the question and decided to answer it by removing the Big Bird head. The guard straightened his uniform and looked up.

"You kids are gonna have to—Huh?"

Rex growled and the guard fainted.

"Come on, Rex!" yelled Davy, as he swung open the big doors.

They moved inside and found themselves in front of a large canoe. There was a gift shop to the left and an entrance to the Imax Theater behind the canoe.

"The offices are down this way," said Davy.

Davy, Rex and Gretchen began walking down a long hallway filled with several displays of insects, with the bugs getting larger as they walked along.

Rex studied each one with interest and began to drool. Davy noticed this and began to get worried.

"I think somebody's hungry. Do you have any candy?"

"How would I have any candy? We didn't go trick or treating."

"Well, we're gonna have to do something. Otherwise, he's gonna try to get into the displays and that's not gonna be pretty."

They passed through the world of insects without incident but as they entered a hallway marked North American Mammals, Rex began to stop and study the larger windows that held a variety of animals, each one looking tastier than the next. Rex tapped on the glass.

"Rex," said Davy. "These aren't real. They're stuffed. Which means, you won't like how they taste.

We'll get you something to eat as soon as we finish up, okay?"

Rex had his eye on a chewy looking rabbit, but sighed and followed Davy along the hallway.

At a police station a few blocks away, an angry looking Professor gathered his belongings and stepped out into the night. Jackson followed right behind him.

"They'll be hearing from the museum about this," muttered the Professor. "Just wait until they want to have a Policeman's Ball in the Rotunda or beneath the giant whale. To treat me like a common criminal."

"Ah, Professor," said Jackson.

"What?" he snapped.

"I wouldn't make too big a stink if I was you."

"Why not?"

"Well, for one, you are sort of a criminal. Peddling dinosaur fossils that really belong to the museum."

"They don't know that."

"They don't now, but if you start making a big thing about getting arrested for trying to saw down a tree in Central Park, they might look a little harder, is all I'm saying."

"Maybe you're right. Come on," said the Professor.

"Where to?" asked Jackson.

"Back to my office."

It took Davy, Gretchen, and Rex a few more minutes to find the Professor's office. It wasn't as close to where his parents worked as Davy had remembered. But finally, they located an office that had the Professor's name on the door.

After several attempts, Davy found the right key and unlocked the office.

Gretchen looked around and saw a lot of fossilized skeletons of different dinosaurs.

"This place gives me the creeps," she said.

Rex saw something across the room and walked over to the Professor's desk. He bent down and looked closer as Davy and Gretchen joined him.

"What is it, Rex?"

Sitting on the desk was a picture of Mount Kilimanjaro and next to it was a map. Rex put his hand on the picture and nodded "yes."

A taxi pulled up in front of the museum and the Professor, followed by Jackson, climbed out. The Professor paid the driver and they climbed the steps to the museum. They were just about to go inside when they saw the guard, who appeared to be sleeping in his guard station. The Professor looked up at the outside of the building and scanned the windows on the second floor.

"What's the matter?" asked Jackson.

"I appear to have visitors," smiled the Professor, as he nodded to a light coming from one of the windows. He took out his cell phone and punched in some numbers.

"Jackson and I are at the museum. Bring the van here and meet us. Now."

He closed up his phone and looked at Jackson.

"One more call," he said, opening the phone up again. He hit a speed dial number. "It's me. How soon can we be ready to go? Really? Is everything ready? I want to move our departure time up. To when? How about tonight?"

Davy and Gretchen studied the map in the Professor's office while Rex licked the picture of Mount Kilimanjaro.

"That's where my parents were last seen," said Davy, pointing to the picture. "I think it's also where he's from," he said, nodding toward Rex.

"Africa's a long way from here," said Gretchen.

"I know," said Davy. "But the Professor said he's putting another expedition together to go back."

"What are you gonna do, follow him?"

"I don't know," admitted Davy. "I just know I have to go there."

Rex heard the sound of footsteps first and let out a low growl.

"What is it, Rex?"

Then Gretchen heard the footsteps.

"Someone's coming," she said.

Davy quickly turned off the light and the room fell into darkness.

The Professor and Jackson tiptoed quietly down the hallway until they came to the Professor's office. They listened at the door, as the Professor gently inserted a key. The door unlocked with the sound of a click and the Professor swung it open.

"Gotcha!" barked the Professor as he turned on the lights and leaped into his office. Only, the office was empty.

"I thought you said you had visitors, Boss," said Jackson as he entered behind the Professor.

"Shhh," said the Professor as he walked to a window that was now wide open. A curtain was blowing in the breeze.

"That window was closed when we were outside," whispered the Professor. He looked out just as Rex, Davy, and Gretchen dropped from a ledge along the outside of the museum to the grassy ground below the Professor's window.

As soon as he hit the grass, Davy looked back up and saw the Professor in the window.

"Give it up, Davy," called the Professor. "You're a smart boy. We can work together on this. Your father would be so proud of you."

"I won't let you hurt him."

"Nobody's going to hurt anyone. I can help you."

"I don't need any help."

"Davy. You're just a boy. You don't understand these things. You're dealing with something that could turn on you at any second. You might think that creature of yours is a friend. It's not, Davy. It's a beast that knows only two things: to kill and to survive. I'm telling you, Davy, for your own good. Get away from it while you can."

A black van pulled up in front of the museum. Out of the rear poured a half dozen men in camouflage, carrying rifles.

From his window, the Professor could see the van arrive, but bushes were blocking Davy's view so he had no idea what was going on. Rex, on the other hand, instinctively sensed the presence of enemies. His nostrils flared and he nudged Davy to stop talking to the Professor and to get them out of there.

"What is it, Rex?"

Rex growled.

"Is somebody coming?"

Rex nodded "yes."

"Davy," said the Professor. "How would you and your friend like to take a little trip?"

"Sounds interesting, Professor, but right now we've gotta be going."

Davy, Rex, and Gretchen began to make their way across the lawn.

The Professor waved to the hunters from the van. "Over here!"

They looked up at him in the window.

"They're right down there!" he screamed, pointing beneath his window. "But they're leaving. Grab them before they get away."

Davy, Gretchen and Rex were halfway across the lawn and heading for 77th Street when they turned and saw the six men running toward them.

"It's those guys from the park again."

Rex bent down and nudged Davy, and then pointed toward his back with his head.

"Are you sure about this?"

Rex nodded "yes."

"Okay," said Davy. "Gretchen, get on," he added as he climbed on Rex's back.

"What are we doing?"

"Just get on. Hurry."

The hunters rounded the corner of the museum and were sprinting across the lawn as Gretchen climbed on Rex's back behind Davy and put her arms around his waist.

As soon as they were on his back, Rex turned and faced the hunters. He then charged at them. The hunters stopped running and looked at the giant Big Bird coming toward them. They were about twenty feet away when Davy yanked the Big Bird head off to reveal a snarling and angry *Tyrannosaurus rex*.

"Oh my God!" screamed one of the hunters.

"I'm not getting paid enough for this stuff," said another, who began running in the other direction. The rest of the hunters quickly tried to aim their weapons.

"Don't anyone dare shoot!" shouted the Professor, who was watching from his window. "The net. Get the net!"

The hunters lowered their weapons and started running for the van, but Rex was right on their tails. He picked one up by the back of his pants and tossed him into the bushes. Another one got to the rear of the van and was about to open the door when he looked up and saw Rex drooling down on him.

"He hasn't had his dinner yet," said Davy.

"Aggghhhhh!" screamed the hunter, who ran off down the street.

Back in his office window, the Professor could see everything. He pounded his fist on the sill in frustration.

"Jackson, would you please get down there and take charge? You've got two children and a baby dinosaur. How hard could this be?"

Jackson looked out the window and saw that Rex, who had ripped his way out of his Big Bird costume, was trying to tip over the van.

"He doesn't look like a baby to me."

"If you need more men, get more men," ordered the Professor. "Now just go down there."

Jackson nodded and left the office.

Rex had the van tilted halfway over when something else caught Davy's attention.

Coming down the middle of 77th Street was a wrestling ring. A wrestling ring? Davy did a double take and then realized that it was actually a wrestling ring on the back of a flatbed truck.

Inside the ring was Davy's favorite wrestler, Dino "the Dinosaur" Dinato wearing the world championship belt. He was there with his manager and a woman wrestler Davy recognized from television.

Rex was still pushing the van. He gave it a final heave and it fell over on its side.

"Follow me!" yelled Davy, as he jumped off of Rex's back, then ran toward the street.

"Where are you going?" said Gretchen as she watched Davy chase after the truck pulling the wrestling ring.

Gretchen and Rex caught up with Davy, but the truck pulling the ring was moving too fast. Davy, Gretchen, and Rex were running as fast as they could but they still couldn't catch up with the wrestling ring.

Back in front of the museum, another truck arrived carrying twenty more hunters, all dressed in black. This group was armed with stun guns, several nets, and prods designed for the capture of large wild animals.

The Professor came out of the museum and climbed into the back of the truck with the new men.

"We're looking for a group of three. A boy and girl, with a rather tall figure wearing either a Big Bird costume or looking like what he really is, a *Tyrannosaurus rex*. Let's move it. They went that way, toward 77th Street."

A group of young men in sweatshirts were pushing boxes of food on dollies into a supermarket on Broadway, when one of them looked up and saw a wrestling ring pass by. This was followed by a group of teenagers on skateboards.

A few seconds later Davy, Gretchen, and Rex were about to run past when Davy noticed the dollies. He stopped running and looked down the street and saw the teenagers on skateboards.

"What's the matter?" asked Gretchen.

"I think I figured out how we can catch the wrestling ring," said Davy.

"Catch the wrestling ring? We're trying to catch a wrestling ring?"

Davy waited until one of the dollies was unloaded, and then ran over and grabbed it before any of the workers noticed it was gone.

"Okay, Rex," said Davy. "Watch how I do this." Davy stood with one foot on the dolly and pushed off with the other.

"Think you can do that?" asked Davy.

Rex shrugged. It looked easy enough.

A clerk inside the store almost dropped the bag of groceries he was packing when he looked out the large front window and saw a boy, a girl, and a dinosaur glide by on one of the store's dollies.

Rex was a natural as he began to weave in and out of traffic, moving closer to the flatbed truck carrying the wrestling ring. Davy looked back and saw a black truck was following them about two blocks behind.

Inside the truck, the Professor lowered his binoculars and tapped on the rear window of the truck cab.

"Faster," he exclaimed. "They're getting away again."

The truck tried to pull out and move ahead in the traffic, but a police car cruised alongside and motioned for it to get back in the proper lane.

The Professor shook his head and took out his cell phone. "Jackson. What's the story with the van?"

Jackson and his men had just turned the van right side up. They climbed inside and sped away from the front of the museum.

"We're all set," said Jackson. "Where to?"

"We're heading down Broadway about two blocks behind a dinosaur on a skateboard," said the Professor. "You can't miss them. I want you to take Columbus and try to cut them off before they get to Columbus Circle."

"Traffic's pretty heavy here, Professor, because of Halloween and all," said Jackson.

"Just do it," said the Professor.

Rex, Davy and Gretchen were gliding along, moving past several cars and trucks when Davy looked back to see if they were still being followed.

"I don't see them," said Davy.

"Maybe we lost them," said Gretchen, hopefully.

"No. He's back there," said Davy. "Try to go a little faster, Rex. If we catch the wrestling ring, you'll be able to hold on to the side and let it pull you along."

"Can I ask a stupid question?" said Gretchen.

"What?"

"Why are we chasing after a wrestling ring?"

"Because the best wrestler in the world is in that ring. And if anyone can help us get away from the Professor, Dino can," said Davy.

"I'm sure," said Gretchen as she rolled her eyes.

Rex was starting to get tired just as they reached the wrestling ring. He held out and grabbed onto the side of the flatbed and let it pull them along.

Dino was talking to his manager when he looked down and saw the dinosaur holding onto the truck with two kids on his back.

"Hey, you," Dino called. "Whatta ya doin?"

He walked over to where they were and knelt down.

"Cool costume," he said to Rex, then added, "but you ain't supposed to be doin' that. You might get hurt or something and then try to sue me."

"We'd never do that," said Davy. "You're my favorite wrestler."

"Oh yeah?" said Dino, smiling and filling his big chest. "You want some candy? Give these kids some candy."

"No, thanks," said Davy.

"I'll take some," said Gretchen, who stuffed a few candy bars in her pockets. "For later," she added.

"You guys headed for the parade, too?" Dino asked.

"Parade?" said Davy. "What parade?"

"The Halloween parade," said Dino. "Why doncha come on up here. You can be a part of my float."

"I got a better idea," said Davy, as he climbed onto the wrestling ring float. He helped Gretchen on and they both pulled Rex aboard.

"What's that, kid?" asked Dino.

"Have you ever wrestled a dinosaur?" asked Davy.

"What? Him?" asked Dino, nodding toward Rex.

"I'd pay to see something like that," said Davy.

"I bet you would, kid," said Dino. "Ya know, that might not be a bad idea. We're always looking for some way to push the envelope, ya know. I mean the Gladiators in Rome did it, right?"

"Did what?" asked Gretchen.

"Fought with animals after people got bored watching them just fight with each other," explained

133

Dino. "Same thing is happening with professional wrestling. It's like you gotta do something more bizarre each time. So wrestling with animals might just be the next cycle. I can dig it," smiled Dino. "And what better animal for Dino to wrestle than a dinosaur, or at least someone dressed like a dinosaur? Okay. You got a deal, kid. But let's wait till we get to the parade. Yeah. I bet we win first prize for sure. 'Dino the Dinosaur' wrestles a dinosaur. You're all right, kid. I tell ya what. You guys are gonna be my guests at the Halloween party after the parade. How's that sound?"

Jackson got out of the van at the corner where Columbus Avenue crossed Broadway at 65th Street. He looked at his watch. "Okay, boys. Take your positions. They oughta be here any minute."

The Professor looked through the binoculars and saw Davy on the flatbed in the wrestling ring talking to someone dressed like a wrestler. He lowered the binoculars and then took out his large needle. He checked to make sure it was full. He picked up the phone. "Jackson, you in position?"

"We're ready, boss," said Jackson.

"They're on some kind of float."

"I see it," said Jackson.

"I want you to pull the van out in front of the street and block them off. Do it now."

"Hey!" said Dino, as he felt the wrestling float jerk to a stop. "What's going on?"

The driver of the float leaned out the window and shouted back.

"Some idiot in a van just blocked the street."

"Go down a side street," said Dino. "I gotta get to the parade before seven or I don't get paid."

Davy looked at Dino. "They're paying you to appear in the parade?" asked Davy.

"You think I'd do this for nothin, kid? Hold on. We're gonna take a detour."

The flatbed truck took a sharp turn and went down 65th Street.

Jackson saw what was happening but there was nothing he could do about it now. He got back in the van and did a U-turn to follow the wrestling ring down 65th Street. The black truck with the Professor continued down Broadway. The Professor picked up his phone.

"Jackson. I thought you said he was cut off."

"You know, it occurs to me that this thing we're following is a parade float."

"So what?"

"Well, if it's for the Halloween parade, then I know where it's going."

"Where's that, Jackson?"

"The Village. They're going to the Village."

"You're sure about that?"

"It's gotta be that. Every Halloween, the Village puts on this big parade."

"Where does it end?" asked the Professor.

"Christopher Street," said Jackson.

"Then get your boys to Christopher Street, Jackson. And wait for us there."

Davy watched as they left the van and the Professor's black truck behind. The driver of the wrestling float went through Central Park and then down Fifth Avenue. They didn't stop until they reached

Washington Square Park, where the Halloween parade was just about to begin.

Dino walked over to Rex and Davy, who had taken position on one corner of the ring.

"Okay, we're just about to start," said Dino. "So you gonna be like his corner man?" he asked Davy.

"Sure," said Davy.

"What am I supposed to do?" asked Gretchen.

"You're gonna be our distraction," said Davy.

"Distraction?" asked Gretchen. "What's that?"

"It's something all wrestlers use to distract their opponents in order to win. Usually they use really good looking women."

"You think I'm good looking?"

"You'll do," said Davy, shyly.

Dino stood in front of Rex and held out his hands to shake.

"I'll try to take it easy on you, big guy," said Dino. "We got the ring well padded so don't be afraid to take a fall. I know this ain't your regular gig, so you just let me do all the work, okay? If you want me to take it easy, just pat me on the back. But I gotta make it look good. Okay. This is gonna be cool. I gotta tell ya. That costume of yours is magnificent. I gotta get one of those for my matches. Come out dressed like a T.rex and then pop out. Wouldn't that be great? You gotta tell me where to get one when we're done. Okay, you ready?"

Rex nodded.

Davy let out a deep sigh.

They were moving through the Village surrounded by other floats and people dressed in elaborate costumes.

CHAPTER FOURTEEN

The Professor checked his watch and then spoke into his phone. He was in the black truck at Washington Square Park. They were at the end of the parade. A man with a clipboard walked by, studying the black truck and looking at the men all dressed in black.

"Very chic," he said, noting something on the clipboard, "but not very original. Next."

The man walked on as the Professor spoke into the phone.

"Jackson, are you ready? No mistakes this time."

"We're all set," answered Jackson, who was parked at the end of Christopher Street. He looked down the street and saw the first floats of the parade round the corner at Seventh Avenue and begin heading toward him.

"Here they come," said Jackson.

Davy was talking to Rex in a corner of the ring, trying to give him wrestling tips. "You gotta watch out for his special move," said Davy. "He gets behind you and puts a sleeper hold on you. He calls it the 'Tyrannosaurus wrecks.' "

"You about ready over there?" shouted Dino from the center of the ring.

"We're ready," said Davy, nodding to the ring announcer, who hit the big silver bell with a metal hammer.

"I want a nice, clean fight," said the referee as he looked back and forth between Rex and Dino. "And if you can't keep it clean, at least make it look good for the crowd lining the street. Just remember, Rex: he puts the sleeper hold on you, you just go out, okay? Don't fight it."

The referee stepped to the side and nodded to the wrestlers. Dino came in low and tried to flip Rex over his knee, but Rex was having none of that. He picked up Dino and body-slammed him into the ring, then sat on him.

Dino squirmed out from under and assumed a defensive pose.

"You've done this before, my friend," smiled Dino. "Let's see you get out of this."

With that, Dino dashed around Rex and grabbed him from behind. He tried to move into position to apply the sleeper, but Rex leaned forward and lifted Dino off the ring. He then did a rolling somersault, taking Dino with him, eventually rolling to a stop against the ropes, with Dino upside down and underneath Rex. Dino's shoulders were pinned to the mat and the ref was just standing there, staring.

Davy yelled from the corner, "Why aren't you counting?"

The ref looked over at Davy. "Cause Dino is supposed to win."

"But Rex has him pinned," insisted Davy.

The ref looked down at Dino, who nodded toward the ropes. The ref noticed that Dino had strategically placed one of his legs over the bottom rope.

"Leg on the rope!" yelled the ref. "You gotta let him up."

Rex seemed confused, but then raised up enough so Dino could squiggle out and stand up.

"You're pretty good, big guy," said Dino, gasping for breath. "You got representation? We could use somebody like you in the wrestling league. Most of the mooks I have to fight are really dinosaurs if you know what I mean. Over the hill, whack jobs. But you got style. We could use some new blood in the ring."

Blood in the ring? Rex didn't like the sound of that.

"Okay, let's wrap this baby up," said Dino as he came in low, going for leverage. As he did, Davy nudged Gretchen, who meandered down the side of the ring so Dino could see her.

"Hey Dino!" shouted Gretchen. "You got a hole in your shorts!"

"Huh?" said Dino as he checked his boxers.

That was all the time Rex needed. He lowered his head and stooped down, coming up behind Dino. He slipped his head between Dino's legs and flipped him over his head. Dino landed on his back and lay there. Rex then climbed up on the top rope before Dino could catch his breath. Rex leaped into the air and jumped onto Dino feet first, then settled down on him while the ref looked on, stunned. The crowd along the parade route was cheering loudly.

"Count!" exclaimed Davy.

The ref counted out, "One! Two! Three!" He then lifted Rex's arm up in victory. "We have a new winner and world champion," proclaimed the ref.

Dino came to his senses and got up off the mat. He didn't look happy as he whispered something to the ref.

"I'm sorry," said the ref to the crowd. "This was not a title match, so the belt remains with Dino the Dinosaur."

The crowd lining the parade route booed and hissed.

Gretchen joined Davy in the corner. "Is that fair?"

Davy was looking at the ref still holding Rex's hand up when he saw what lay ahead at the end of Christopher Street. The van Rex had tipped over was now parked at the corner of Christopher and West streets. Davy couldn't see the Professor but he knew he must be close by. He tapped Rex on the back and nodded to Gretchen.

"Come on," said Davy. "We have to get off here."

"But they haven't judged the float yet," said Gretchen. "Here come the judges now."

"The Professor's men are here," said Davy. "If we don't go now, it will be too late."

Davy, Rex, and Gretchen slipped off the float and into the crowd on the sidewalk lining Christopher Street just as the man with the clipboard approached the wrestling ring.

"Hey," shouted Dino as he saw Davy, Rex, and Gretchen were about to slip into the crowd. "Don't leave now. They haven't given out the prizes yet. Get back here."

"Well, well," said the man with the clipboard. "A wrestling ring. And a real wrestler. I'm underwhelmed."

Davy heard what the judge said and stopped. He pulled Rex and Gretchen back to the ring. "We're with him," said Davy to the judge as he joined Dino in the ring.

Dino smiled and struck a pose next to Rex, who also struck a wrestling pose.

Photographers snapped pictures and the judge nodded. "Okay. You win."

Dino smiled and turned to thank his new friends, but they had already left the ring.

Jackson was watching closely as each float passed by on to its final stop on the river at West and Christopher streets. He nudged one of his men when a float with a large dog passed by.

"Check out the dog," Jackson ordered. "He might have changed costumes."

The hunter jumped onto the float and sneaked up behind the large dog. He slowly reached out and grabbed the dog's head from behind and, with a quick motion, yanked it upward. The head came off easily, revealing the dazed head of a rather large man underneath.

"Hey! Who took my head?" shouted the man in the dog costume.

Jackson was starting to look concerned as he walked through the parade watchers and along the floats.

"He's got to be here," said Jackson as a chill ran down his spine. There, just ahead of him, in the black truck, was the Professor and his group. Oh boy, thought Jackson.

Just then the float with the wrestling ring started to pass by. Jackson reached out and pulled Dino off the float.

"Take it easy!" said Dino. "Just because we fight in the ring, doesn't mean we like to fight everybody we see."

"I'm looking for a kid and a dinosaur," said Jackson. "You see anything like that?"

"Oh yeah. Best costume in the parade," said Dino. "He helped me win First Prize for the float. Has a mean suplex, too."

"Where are they?" asked Jackson.

"I don't know," said Dino. "They split before I could thank them."

"What do you mean? They left the parade?"

"I'll probably see them later at the party," said Dino.

"Party?" said Jackson. "What party?"

"Monster Halloween Party, man. Best party in the Village," said Dino "Over on Jane Street. You can't miss it."

"Thanks," said Jackson, just as the Professor pulled up in his truck. The Professor jumped to the street and went directly to Jackson.

"Tell me you have them," said the Professor.

"I know where they're going to be," said Jackson, smiling.

The multi-floored disco dance club was filled with people in outrageous costumes. A huge dance floor with pulsating lights and music was packed with dancers in all sizes and shapes. In the center of the floor, Rex was dancing with a woman wrestler from the wrestling ring. She couldn't keep her hands off Rex's soft, leathery skin.

"You have to tell me where you got this leather," she said. "It's just so soft and warm. It feels almost alive!"

Sitting in a balcony, high above the dance floor, Davy and Gretchen were at a table talking and looking down at Rex dancing and keeping time with the disco beat.

"Look at him down there," said Davy.

"The dude can move," said Gretchen, tapping her feet to the music. She felt Davy's eyes on her and she looked at him across the table.

"What?" she said.

"I don't know what to do," said Davy.

"What do you want to do?" she asked.

"Find someplace where he can just be himself. Where he doesn't have to hide all the time," said Davy.

"He looks like he's enjoying himself."

"Then there's the Professor. What am I gonna do about him?"

Gretchen reached across the table and took Davy's hand.

"You'll figure something out," she said. "You've done pretty good so far."

"What if I've just been lucky? What if my luck is running out?"

Gretchen leaned across the table and kissed Davy on the lips. This caused him to look wide-eyed at Gretchen. "Come on, tough guy. Let's dance."

Rex was still dancing with the woman when Gretchen and Davy joined them on the floor. Rex picked up the wrestling lady and swung her around and down and through his legs. Just then, across the floor, a door opened and in stepped the Professor and his hunters.

Davy and Gretchen were dancing when Davy saw Jackson making his way through the crowd on the dance floor. Davy then turned and saw the Professor pushing his way through as well. Gretchen looked at Davy and then at the Professor. Gretchen put her mouth to Davy's ear.

"Time for another distraction," she said.

"Wait," said Davy. "What are you gonna do?"

Gretchen stopped dancing and began to back off the floor.

"Gretchen!" shouted Davy. "Be careful."

Gretchen backed into the crowded floor and disappeared as the Professor and his men surrounded Davy and Rex on the dance floor. Rex realized something had changed and put the wrestling woman down. Davy moved next to Rex.

"He has to leave now," said Davy.

"Come on, kid," said the woman. "We're just getting friendly."

"But we have to go," said Davy. "I know Rex really likes you, but it could get a little rough in here. You better get off the dance floor."

"You think I can't take care of myself?" said the woman wrestler. "I'm just as good as Dino. In fact, I'm the women's wrestling champion."

The Professor and Jackson, along with about a dozen hunters, closed the circle until the only ones inside the circle were Rex, Davy, and the woman wrestler.

A hunter grabbed her by the arm and started to pull her away. She, in turn, picked up the hunter and body-slammed him in the middle of the dance floor. Just then

Dino showed up and pushed his way to the dance floor and walked over to Rex.

"Hey, what's going on, big guy? These people giving you a hard time?"

"Something funny's going on here, Dino," said the woman wrestler.

Rex started to move toward another hunter, who backed away.

The Professor stepped forward, staring at Rex in wonder. He couldn't believe his eyes. He almost wanted to cry.

"What a perfect specimen," he said. "Davy. You are to be commended. He's in excellent condition."

"I won't let you hurt him," snapped Davy.

"No one's going to hurt him," said the Professor.

"Who's this guy?" asked Dino. "You bothering my friends, here?"

The Professor reached into the pocket of his coat, felt the needle slide into his hand, and took a step forward. Suddenly, the lights went out. Standing in the corner in the dark, Gretchen had a fuse box opened and had thrown the main switch. People stopped dancing and started screaming. Many of them began running toward the doors and shouting.

The bodies of hunters began flying through the air. Rex, Dino, and the woman wrestler were beating up the Professor's men. Davy made his way over to Rex and whispered in his ear. "Follow me."

"Seal the exits!" shouted the Professor. "Don't let him get away!"

Suddenly, the lights came back on. The Professor was standing next to one of the hunters lying unconscious on the dance floor. Dino was next to him, asleep, with a needle in his arm. The Professor removed his needle and put it back in his pocket. He looked around at where Davy and Rex had been standing and they were gone. The Professor began pushing his way through the remaining dancers.

Rex and Davy were outside, climbing down a fire escape behind the building. They dropped the final floor into an alley way and ran toward Jane Street.

"This way," said Davy, as he and Rex started to leave the alley. They got about halfway down the alley when a door opened in a wall and the Professor stepped out, holding his needle. This time he didn't hesitate. He plunged the needle into Rex's side. Rex looked down and then looked at Davy.

"No!" screamed Davy.

Rex reached down and pulled out the needle. He then opened his mouth and was about to roar at the Professor, but then something happened. Rex's mouth wouldn't move. It just hung open, with his tongue hanging out. He reached out to hold onto something, gave Davy a confused look and then toppled over on his side.

"Sleep tight, big fella," said the Professor as he nudged the sleeping dinosaur.

Davy looked horrified as he stared at Rex lying in the alley.

"Rex!" he shouted as he tried to go to the dinosaur, but Jackson grabbed him from behind and lifted him up, kicking, off the pavement.

"What do you want me to do with this kid?" Jackson asked the Professor.

"I'm afraid he's going to have to come with us. He knows too much," said the Professor. "Come on. Let's get out of here before we have visitors." Three of the hunters draped a large canvas tarp over Rex while a dozen others lifted him up and carried him to the flatbed truck.

"What are you going to do with Rex?" asked Davy.

"We're going to take a little trip, young Mr. Ross," said the Professor.

When Davy still hadn't returned home from trick or treating by 11:30, Rebecca Ross started to panic. She couldn't go out looking for him because he might come back while she was out so she called the local precinct. The desk sergeant said they would send two detectives over to get a recent photograph of Davy.

Grandma Becky could feel her heart pounding when the front door buzzed.

She ran to the door and opened it, expecting to see the two detectives. Instead, she found a woman in her early 40s with bleached blonde hair and too much makeup.

"Yes?" said Grandma Becky.

"My name's Charlotte Tucker. My daughter Gretchen said she was going trick or treating with a Davy Ross. She gave me this address. I thought she'd be home by now. I was out, you see, and when I got home, she wasn't there. I tried calling, but your line was busy. I normally wouldn't have bothered to track her down, but I was planning to take a short trip and wanted to let her know. I hope I'm not intruding. Is she here?"

"Oh dear," said Grandma Becky. "Why don't you come in and sit down. The police are on the way."

"The police? What has she done now?"

CHAPTER FIFTEEN

A cargo plane sat on an empty runway. Men loaded supplies into the belly of the plane. Davy sat in the van with Jackson staring out the passenger window watching workmen load a large crate onto the airplane. He wondered if Rex was inside. He wished he could go and check on him to make sure he was okay, but Jackson had tied Davy's hands and feet together after he tried to escape.

Davy saw the Professor checking the crate, making sure it was in place and secured. He nodded to someone in the cockpit and the large door in the rear of the plane began to close.

The Professor then gave the word to take off and he climbed aboard the passenger part of the cargo plane. Jackson looked at Davy.

"Are you gonna give me any trouble?"

Davy shook his head no.

"Okay," said Jackson, "because, we're gonna get on that plane. I don't feel like carrying you but I will if I have to. So I'm gonna untie your feet. Now just so we understand each other, if it was up to me, I'd finish you off right here. Know what I'm saying? To me, you're just a pain in the neck. Nothing but trouble. Who needs you? But the Professor has it in his mind to take you along. He thinks you might be useful on the other end. Why, I don't know. So all I want you to know is that I would think nothing about putting you down right here. I just want you to know that in case you was thinking about trying something stupid. Are we clear on that?"

Davy nodded yes.

"Okay, let's go then," said Jackson as he took out a knife and sliced the cord around Davy's feet. Jackson slid out of the van and led Davy to the cargo plane. They climbed the ladder to the passenger section and the door closed behind them.

The cargo door was still closing in the rear. Before it finished closing, a figure dashed out of the darkness and slipped into the cargo hold just as the big door clicked shut. Inside the door, Gretchen caught her breath. She looked around in the darkness and listened to the sound of snoring.

The plane began to taxi down the runway. At the end, it turned around and the pilot fired the jets. The plane sped back down the runway and took off into the night sky.

As the plane climbed to cruising altitude, the Professor got up from his seat and walked back down the aisle. He took a seat next to Davy, who was now re-bound and gagged. The Professor removed the gag.

"No need for this anymore," said the Professor. "I don't think Jackson likes you."

"I don't like him either, so we're even," said Davy.

"Even?" said the Professor. "I don't think so. Jackson is a professional soldier. A mercenary. He knows a hundred different ways to kill somebody."

"He wouldn't be so tough if Rex was here. What have you done to him?"

"Just a mild tranquilizer," said the Professor. "Well, I suppose 'mild' is a relative term. He'll be fine."

"Please don't kill Rex," begged Davy. "You were wrong, you know. Dinosaurs and people can get along just fine."

"I'm not going to kill Rex," said the Professor.

"But you said dinosaurs and man couldn't co-exist."

"Well I guess you proved me wrong, didn't you Davy. We have so much to learn. This is just the beginning."

"What are you doing? Where are we going?"

"Africa."

"Mount Kilimanjaro?"

"That's right."

"Are we going to look for my parents?"

"We could," said the Professor. "But mainly we're going to see if there are any more Rexes."

Meanwhile, in the cargo hold Gretchen was looking for something. She found it under some blankets. She lifted the crowbar and went to the crate. Wedging it in between the opening, she pushed with all her weight. Nothing. She looked around some more and found an axe. She went back to the crate and began to chop. She got a couple of pieces of wood off, but stopped. Beneath the wood were metal bars. She reached in and found the sleeping dinosaur. She petted the animal's back and slumped to the floor next to the crate.

"We'll think of something, Rex."

Davy stared out the window at the night sky above the clouds. A thought flashed through his mind and he turned back toward the Professor.

"You're going to use Rex to lead you to them," said Davy.

"Excellent deduction. You have your parents' brains. What better way? It's like a built-in homing device. If anyone knows where to look, it's Rex."

"What if you do find more?"

"Well, then we'll have a hard decision to make."

"What kind of decision?"

"What would make the most sense financially. I mean, Rex is supposed to be extinct, but if there are a few thousand more of him running around, suddenly his value is diminished drastically. But if he's only one of a few, then that would be great."

"You mean if you find lots of dinosaurs, you're going to destroy them?"

"It's just business, Davy. We have to control our market. I don't know why I'm trying to convince you. Your parents never understood what I was doing, either. I could have made them rich. They'd probably still be alive today, but all they wanted to do was play scientist. Look where that got them. What am I going to do with you, Davy? You're the only loose end."

The Professor got up and walked off down the aisle. A chill ran down Davy's back as he stared out into the darkness and tried to relax enough to sleep. He would need his rest if he were going to save Rex.

The plane zoomed across the sky. The Professor looked out at the sun rising on the eastern horizon. Far in the distance, he could almost see the tops of a large mountain range.

Down in the cargo hold, Gretchen was asleep next to the crate. She had removed enough of the wood so that some of Rex could be seen through the bars underneath. What no one could see, however, was how much Rex had grown during the flight. At nearly ten feet, he now barely fit inside the cramped space of the cage.

Rex had been asleep since being drugged after the dance. It was a struggle, but he managed to open one eye. All he could see was a steel bar and a narrow opening in the wood crate. He tried to move but there no longer was any space. This was a new sensation for him. He had never been restrained before in his life. He didn't like it. He had to get out of this place. It was hard for him to breathe. He tried to open his mouth, but someone had tied it shut. He tried to raise his head, but it barely moved, maybe an inch at most, before it fell back to the floor of the metal cage.

Still, the faint vibration was enough to wake Gretchen, who reached through the bars and stroked Rex's nose.

"Rex. Are you awake in there?"

Rex recognized the scent first, and then the voice.

All Rex could do was moan a mournful, painful sound.

"It's gonna be all right," said Gretchen. "I'm gonna get you out of there, but I need your help."

Davy stared out the window of the plane. He thought of his grandmother and felt bad about how worried she must be. He didn't know if he had slept at all, or if he was dreaming when he saw a valley appear in the clouds. The plane passed over the valley and began its descent down through the clouds.

Davy had the feeling that what he had just seen was very special. He turned away from the window as the Professor took the seat next to him.

"We'll be landing soon. Davy," he said. "But then we'll have about half-a-day's journey by truck back up the mountain and then another half-mile on foot. I'd like to bring you along, but you could cause trouble. Jackson thinks I should leave you with the plane."

"Come on, Professor. I'm eleven years old. How much trouble could I be?"

"You've already proven to be very resourceful."

"Well, then wouldn't you want me where you could see me?"

"Good point. Fasten your seat belt."

CHAPTER SIXTEEN

The cargo plane landed on an airstrip that looked like it had been cut out of the middle of a jungle. There was just enough open space for the plane to land and turn around. The rest was thick jungle in every direction.

The plane taxied to a stop and a flatbed truck backed up to the cargo hatch as it opened. A group of men entered the cargo hold and began removing supplies. A forklift drove up the entranceway and positioned itself before the crate. The boards Gretchen had pried off were now back in place. There was no sign of Gretchen. The forklift picked up the crate and carried it off the plane, depositing it on the rear of the flatbed truck.

The Professor led Davy to the truck's cab, while the other men followed Jackson to another truck parked next to the flatbed. Jackson gave a signal and the first truck pulled away while the Professor and Davy followed in the flatbed.

"I thought it best if I kept you and Jackson apart," said the Professor.

"Where are we going?" asked Davy.

"You saw it when we flew in. The valley in the clouds."

The two trucks moved along a steep, winding, mountainous jungle road. Davy could look out the window and see the sheer drop. The wheels of the truck barely fit on the road. One wrong turn and the truck would go over the cliff. Davy hoped the driver knew where he was going.

He looked ahead at the lead truck, which was one of those troop carriers. It was covered in the back where men sat on rows along each side. Jackson was in the rear staring back at him. Davy looked away and then turned toward the rearview mirror. He could see a corner of the crate tied to the flatbed. He wanted to see if Rex was okay. He figured Rex must really be hungry.

A feeling of sadness passed through him. How was he going to help his friend? It seemed useless. He was almost ready to admit defeat when he saw a movement in the rearview mirror. He looked again and to his amazement, he saw Gretchen stick her head out from behind the crate.

How did she get here? he wondered. Then he saw something that suddenly changed everything. Out from behind the crate appeared first a hand and then a shoulder, and finally, the head of a ten-foot *Tyrannosaurus.*

Gretchen climbed on Rex's back and they leaped off the rear of the flatbed. Davy watched in amazement as they disappeared into the jungle. Davy looked over at the Professor, who was studying a map, when the truck started to slow down.

The Professor turned toward the driver. "What are you doing?"

"I felt something," said the driver. "I just want to check it out."

The truck stopped and the driver got out.

"I'd better take a look, too," said the Professor as he began to slide across the seat to climb out. He was at the door when he turned around. "Aren't you coming?"

"I'll wait here," said Davy.

"You'll come with me," ordered the Professor. Davy complied by sliding across the seat and following him onto the road. It took them longer than usual to walk back to the flatbed because there wasn't much room between the truck and the edge of the cliff. Meanwhile, Jackson was climbing out of the rear of the lead truck to join them.

The driver reached the rear of the flatbed first and he was staring at the crate when the Professor and Davy walked up to him.

"What is it?" asked the Professor.

The driver continued to stare at the crate, speechless. Davy and the Professor noticed it at the same time. The far side of the crate was torn open, with boards hanging loose and metal bars bent open.

Jackson reached them and looked at the crate. He jumped onto the flatbed and looked inside the crate. He then entered through the opening and bent down.

When he returned, Jackson was holding something in his hand.

"Look what I found," said Jackson, holding out his hand, which contained a wrinkled and empty wrapper from a candy bar.

"It appears we have a stowaway," said the Professor.

"I better get the men," said Jackson. "They can't be too far away."

"Take your time," said the Professor. "We know where they're going."

"Right," said Jackson, who snickered at Davy as he walked away.

Davy knew something was wrong. Why wasn't the Professor more upset? He should be jumping up and down, and screaming by now.

The Professor knelt down and faced Davy. He took something out of his pocket. It looked like a compass with an arrow and a flashing light.

"Know what this is, Davy?"

"What?"

"It's a tracking receiver. You know what's making that light blink and that arrow move?"

"Rex?"

"Looks like he's headed up the mountain. I bet that girl I saw you with is there, too," said the Professor. "Come on, Davy. Let's get in the truck. We don't want to still be driving on this road at night."

Davy looked out over the cliff and saw the drop was about 500 feet straight down. "I don't want to be driving on this road in daylight," Davy said to himself.

About a half-mile away, Rex and Gretchen plowed through the thick jungle foliage, with Rex making his own trail.

"Take it easy, Rex," said Gretchen. "Do you even know where you're going?"

Rex nodded "yes."

"I don't want to get lost. We have to go back and help Davy," said Gretchen.

Rex nodded "yes" again.

"Well, then why are we going this way?" she asked. "We're getting farther and farther away from him."

Rex shook his head "no" and continued on into the dense green jungle.

Neither Rex nor Gretchen had noticed the tiny metal device wedged between the first and second toes of Rex's left foot. As Rex plowed though the jungle, you could just barely see the small red light blinking between the dinosaur's toes.

The trucks were moving again up the steep and curvy mountain road. They went about another quarter mile when the road ended. It just stopped and all that there was leading the rest of the way up the mountain was a narrow dirt walking path.

The trucks stopped and everyone got out.

The Professor looked around as Davy climbed out of the truck and saw the top of the mountain disappear among the clouds.

"This is it. Magnificent, isn't it, Davy?"

"Is this where my mother and father were?" asked Davy as he let out a sigh.

"Right up there," said the Professor, pointing up through the clouds.

Professor Berenson looked at his tracking device.

"Your friend moves pretty fast," said the Professor. "Look. He's already up there."

"What's gonna happen to Rex?"

"Don't worry about Rex, Davy. He's gonna be fine. There's a collector in Fiji who's paying ten million dollars for him. I'm sure he'll be well taken care of."

Davy looked around at the jungle and the mountain. He sensed something.

"Professor," said Davy. "You're forgetting about something that's real important."

"What's that, Davy?"

"Rex might not want to go to Fiji. I can tell you—if Rex doesn't want to do something, he ain't gonna do it."

"You let me worry about that," said the Professor. "Come on. We're almost there."

The Professor took Davy by the arm and led him down the path.

They walked through thick jungle for about half a mile until the path opened into a clearing. It was the same spot on which Sam and Margaret Ross had pitched their campsite, only now there wasn't any sign that a camp had once stood on this spot.

Davy looked out over the valley that was in the clouds and had a sense of déjà vu even though he had never seen this place before. He knew it had special meaning. He looked around the clearing that was filling with men carrying tents and supplies. Jackson was organizing a crew to set up camp. Davy walked to the edge of the clearing where a cliff dropped hundreds of feet to a jungle valley below.

The Professor gripped Jackson by the arm and took him aside.

"Place the charges in exactly the same place," said the Professor. "I want you to replicate the explosion as closely as possible."

"You think that's a good idea?" asked Jackson.

"Got a better one?" challenged the Professor.

"What if it causes another landslide?"

"I'm counting on it," said the Professor. "Only this time we'll be ready."

"Seems kind of risky," said Jackson.

"A life without risk isn't worth living," said the Professor. "Let's get moving."

"You're nuts," Jackson mumbled to himself after the Professor had walked away.

Davy walked along the edge of the cliff looking out over the valley and through the clouds. He tried to see beneath the clouds, but they were too thick and covered the valley like a warm blanket.

As Davy stared down, a fog began rolling in around the edge of the cliff and through the jungle. The Professor looked up from his notes and saw the fog. He checked his tracking device and saw that the arrow appeared to be frozen. He turned the device around but the arrow stayed in the same position no matter which way the Professor pointed the device. He looked down at the ground with a perplexed expression on his face.

"That's strange," said the Professor.

"What's strange?" asked Jackson.

"According to the tracking device, our dinosaur should be standing right where I am," said the Professor. "Unless he's—" The Professor and Jackson looked down at the same time. "—underground."

Jackson and the Professor looked up at each other.

"Shut off the timer!" shouted the Professor.

"We may be a little—" The explosion cut off Jackson's sentence and sent them flying through the air. "—late," Jackson added as he landed in a heap. Suddenly, the ground began to shake.

"That's it!"

"That's what?"

"The mountain must be hollow," said the Professor. "What am I thinking about? Of course it's hollow. Mount Kilimanjaro is a dormant volcano. Watch for the cracks."

Davy was clinging to a vine as the ground shuddered around him. Suddenly, a crack started to appear in the ground, beginning in the jungle and then running out to the edge where Davy was standing.

"Aggghhhh!" screamed Davy.

Davy pulled himself up on the vine when the ground opened up under him. He was holding on when he thought he heard Gretchen say, "Davy. Let go."

Davy looked confused.

"Gretchen?"

"Let go, Davy," said the voice again.

"I can't," pleaded Davy, looking down into the darkness of the crack in the earth. The Professor scanned the area and saw Davy hanging on the vine. Fog and dust were starting to block everything out.

"Jackson! Have your men bring the rope and the wedges," ordered the Professor.

As the crack opened wider, men started inserting large wedge-like objects. Davy was surrounded by fog and couldn't see anything.

"There's somebody down here who really wants to see you," said Gretchen.

"I still can't see anything," said Davy.

"You have to trust me, Davy. Just jump."

"Hey!" shouted the Professor. "You better get over here, Davy. It looks like another earthquake. Stay next to me."

Davy was torn. He looked down into the fog, trying as hard as he could to see, but still saw nothing. Then he saw Jackson coming toward him and he made a decision. He closed his eyes and let go, falling into the crack.

He felt them before he could see them. When Davy opened his eyes he saw a pair of dinosaur arms was holding him. Rex's head, which had gotten even bigger during the trip, poked through the fog.

"Rex!" screamed Davy with joy in his voice.

Rex had managed to climb up the crack by bracing himself against the two sides. He was now lowering himself and Davy back down through the crevice.

"I never thought I'd see you again," said Davy.

Rex reached the bottom, which was part of a huge cavern that opened out into another jungle that lay hidden beneath the cloud cover. Rex put Davy down and Davy saw the blinking red light of the tracking device wedged between Rex's toes. He reached down, removed the device and then crushed it under his foot as Gretchen stepped out of the shadows, smiling.

"What are you doing?"

"Give us some time," said Davy.

"Isn't this place great? Wait till you see the size of the trees down here," she said, taking Davy's hand.

Meanwhile, back on the top, the Professor noticed the light had gone out on the tracking device.

"Come on," the Professor yelled to Jackson. "Into the crevice. Hurry!"

Jackson looked down into the fog coming from the crack in the earth.

"You want me to go down there?"

"That's where the boy went. I bet that's where Rex is, too. Now get moving."

"After you, Professor," said Jackson.

"If you want your pay, Jackson, you'll do as I say," ordered the Professor. "Now you and your men get down inside that crevice and report back to me."

Jackson glared at the Professor but then gave in and nodded to his men to follow him.

Davy looked up and saw several men with ropes and weapons climbing down through the fog in the crevice.

"We gotta get outta here," said Davy.

Rex snarled and started to wander off into the darkness.

"Rex? Where are you going?" asked Davy, as he chased after him. Gretchen followed right behind them. Davy looked back and saw Jackson drop into the cavern. Jackson looked up and saw Davy. He smiled and waved to him. Davy shook his head and took off again after Rex.

As they ran through the hidden jungle, Davy turned to Gretchen and asked, "How did you two get down here? How did you know about this place?"

"I didn't. Rex did," Gretchen said smiling. "Oh, Davy, you ain't seen nuthin."

Jackson gathered his men together and waited as the Professor lowered himself by a rope to the cavern floor. He looked around in wonder.

"Do you smell it, Jackson?"

"Smell what?"

"That musty smell. It's everywhere. It's the same smell as the egg. It's the smell of another world. Did you see which way they went?"

"That way," pointed Jackson.

"Let's go," said the Professor.

Davy, Rex, and Gretchen made their way along a narrow ledge. Davy looked down to find himself on the side of a huge underground cliff inside a giant hallway.

"Try not to look down," said Gretchen.

"Good idea," said Davy, so he looked out over the huge room and continued following Rex along the narrow ledge.

"Do you know where we're going?"

"You'll see," smiled Gretchen.

Davy almost slipped but Gretchen grabbed him. He looked down and couldn't see the bottom. If he fell, it would have been into oblivion.

"Oh, boy," said Davy.

"Be careful," said Gretchen.

They finally came to the end of the ledge and were now looking down into a huge valley. Gretchen waited for Davy to reach her and as he looked down his face widened in wonder. Before them, stretching as far as the eye could see, was an underground world where several dozen dinosaurs in all shapes and sizes were grazing in the distance. There was a family of *Apatosaurus*es grazing near a stream. Two baby *Stegosaurus*es were playing in a field. Nearby, a *Triceratops* scratched its back on a tree trunk.

"Holy cow!" said Davy.

At the end of the ledge was a long, natural slide made in the side of the cliff. Rex nodded to the slide, which reminded Davy of the big slide in Central Park. Rex playfully slid down, followed by Gretchen and Davy.

CHAPTER SEVENTEEN

At the bottom of the slide, an *Allosaurus* walked over and sniffed Davy and put its head down and Davy petted it. Suddenly, Davy looked alarmed.

"What's the matter?"

"We have to stop him."

"Who?"

"The Professor. He's going to sell them."

"Sell who?"

"The dinosaurs."

"How? He doesn't even own them," said Gretchen. "Nobody does."

"But that's why he's here. He's already got a buyer for Rex. He sold him for ten million dollars and he doesn't own Rex. He used Rex the same way he used my parents. He's either going to sell them or kill them. I think he had my parents killed too."

"The Professor!"

"He had one of his men, that Jackson character, try to scare them so they would leave and then Jackson would come in and steal whatever they found in their dig. Only something went wrong. Jackson set an explosion and it caused the earthquake and landslide. He killed my parents and when he gets his dinosaurs, he's probably going to kill us."

"We can't let him do that, can we?" said a man's voice.

Davy whirled around and saw the outline of a man and a woman stepping toward him through the mist. The couple was wearing worn clothing and looked a little like cave people. The man had a long beard and the woman had a touch of gray in her hair, but as they moved closer, Davy got a better look and he realized who they were.

"Mom? Dad?"

"Davy? Is that you?" asked Sam as he and his wife stepped into the light.

Davy couldn't believe his eyes.

"Davy!" cried Margaret Ross as she ran to her son. She picked him up and gave him a big hug. Sam Ross joined his wife and smiled at Davy.

"You're alive!" said Davy.

"How did you find us?" asked Sam.

"Rex."

"Who's Rex?" asked Margaret, setting Davy down.

Just then Rex ambled over and licked Davy's arm.

"You sent him to me, remember?"

Sam and Margaret looked at each other and spoke at the same time. "The egg!"

Sam walked over to Rex and let Rex smell him. "So that's where it went." He patted Rex's head.

"If you were alive all this time, why didn't you come home?"

"We tried, Davy. We've been looking for a way out since we fell down here. But after the earthquake, the crevices sealed back up. We've looked everywhere. Meanwhile, we just tried to stay alive, eating plants and fruits. The amazing thing is the dinosaurs pretty much ignored us. Even the predators. We'd almost resigned ourselves to the possibility that we were going to be here forever when we heard the explosions and followed the sound. Then you appeared."

"Rex will show us the way out," said Davy. "Won't you, Rex?"

Rex smiled his crooked smile and nodded "yes."

"I just can't believe you're here. How did you even get to Africa?"

Before Davy could answer, a couple of stones rolled down the slide and Davy looked up to see the Professor, Jackson, and the rest of his men.

"Mr. and Mrs. Ross. What an unpleasant surprise," said the Professor as he and the others slid down the slide.

"Berenson," said Sam. He turned to Davy. "Don't tell me you brought Berenson with you?"

"Well, he sorta brought me," said Davy, feeling embarrassed.

Jackson and his men surrounded Davy, Gretchen, Sam, Margaret, and Rex. They were all armed with either machine guns or strange looking dart guns. Professor Berenson approached the group.

"Well, well. This certainly complicates things," said the Professor. "We assumed you were dead."

"I bet you did," said Sam. "I overheard my son talking about how one of your men set off the explosion that caused the earthquake."

"That was an accident. We just wanted you out of here once you found the valley," said the Professor. "I told you and Margaret how much money could be made. Dinosaur fossils are big business. Getting bigger all the time. Do you really think the museum cares how many *Pterodactyl* wings it has? But some collectors can't get enough of them. We don't have to have this discussion again, do we? Even you must see the opportunity here."

"You're nothing but a fence, Berenson," snapped Sam.

"And about to become quite a rich one. Jackson, the net."

Jackson and his men unfurled a large net and surrounded Rex.

"It was this fine young specimen who led us to you," said the Professor, nodding toward Rex. "Your son did a magnificent job raising him in what must have been extremely difficult circumstances. I mean, the upper West Side of Manhattan isn't what I'd call an optimum environment for the care and feeding of extinct creatures such as this."

"He's gonna sell Rex for ten million dollars," said Davy.

"You're a disgrace to paleontology, Berenson," said Sam Ross.

"I wish there was some other way to do this," said the Professor as he shook his head. "I really do. But you would never see things my way, and this is just too great an opportunity to let a couple of second-rate scientists stand in the way of exploiting the discovery of a lifetime. I'm truly sorry."

He nodded to Jackson.

"Professor?" asked Jackson.

"It's time to finish the job you started."

Jackson looked at the Professor.

"What? You want me to kill them?"

"Technically, you've already done that."

"But that was an accident," said Jackson.

"Are you going soft on me, Jackson?" snarled the Professor.

"No. It's just—"

"You're a soldier. Pretend you're at war. They're the enemy standing between you and millions of dollars. Come on. We don't have all day. We have buyers waiting."

Jackson shouldered his weapon and put his finger on the trigger. His forehead was covered with sweat. He looked through his scope and saw Davy looking back at him. Then Sam Ross stepped forward and stood in front of his family.

"You can't do this," said Sam.

Jackson could feel the sweat trickle into his eyes. He felt the trigger against his finger. Just a few pounds of pressure. All he had to do was squeeze and he'd kill the father and son with one bullet. Only he couldn't do it. Jackson wiped the sweat from his eyes and lowered his rifle.

"What are you doing?" said the Professor.

"He's right," said Jackson. "There's gotta be a better way. I ain't killing anyone in cold blood. Why can't we just leave them here?"

169

Professor Berenson walked over to Jackson.

"Give me that gun!" he screamed. He snatched the weapon out of Jackson's hand when the cavern began to shake.

"What the hell?" said the Professor.

A loud roar thundered through the cavern, making the ground shake. The men holding the net looked up just as the largest *Tyrannosaurus rex* that ever lived poked its head over some rocks. It then bent down and moved into the space that had been large but was now quite crowded with the presence of the huge, angry beast.

The Professor aimed the gun at the 45-foot tall dinosaur and was about to fire when Sam dove toward him and in a flying tackle knocked the Professor to the ground. A burst of machine gun fire went wild.

The huge T.rex let out an angry roar.

The Professor tried to get off another shot but Sam pinned his arms and hand to the ground.

"I wouldn't do that if I were you," said Sam. "She's already angry over you trying to take her son away."

The Professor looked over toward the dinosaur.

"What are you talking about? Are you trying to tell me that thing is Rex's mother?"

"Can't you see the resemblance?"

"So what if she is? Even you should know there's never been any proof that dinosaurs cared for their young."

"Oh, I think we're about to witness some of that proof right now," said Sam.

"Jackson," shouted the Professor. "The dart gun. Shoot that thing!"

Jackson took the dart gun from one of his men and aimed at the mother T.rex. But before he could fire, the huge creature slammed the side of the cavern with her mighty tail, causing a vibration so strong it knocked Jackson down.

Sam was watching Jackson and not paying attention to the Professor as he eased his machine gun into a swinging position.

"I don't think Rex's Mom is going to let anything happen to—"

Before Sam could finish, the Professor slammed him in the back of the head with the wooden stock of his machine gun, knocking Sam unconscious.

The Professor pushed Sam aside and stood up. He pointed the gun down at Sam.

"Rex!" screamed Davy.

The Professor was about to fire when he felt himself being lifted from behind. He turned his head to see Rex holding him off the ground. Before he could react, Rex body-slammed the Professor onto the floor of the cavern.

"Way to go, Rex!" screamed Davy.

"Jackson!" exclaimed the Professor. "Help me."

Jackson began to back away, putting his hands up in front of him defensively.

"Hey! Where are you going?" shouted the Professor.

"You're on your own, Professor," said Jackson. "You don't pay me enough for this. I quit."

With that, he and his men ran from the cavern.

The Professor glared up at Rex. "You think this is over?"

The Professor reached into his coat and pulled out his tranquilizer needle.

Davy saw what was about to happen.

"Rex! Get back!"

Rex moved out of the way just as the Professor tried to stab him with the needle. When the Professor looked up, he saw a shadow falling over him. At first he thought he was looking a giant moving cave getting closer and closer. Only instead of stalagmites and stalactites, the cave had huge, sharp teeth around the opening. Suddenly he realized this was not a cave but the mouth of Rex's mother.

The Professor tried to move as huge gob of saliva dripped down around him.

"Get away from me!" shouted the Professor. He looked over at Sam who was just regaining his consciousness. "Sam! Tell it to get back. Tell it now, Sam!"

"I don't know, Professor," said Sam. "You were about to stick her son with a needle."

"No!" screamed the Professor as the mouth of the mother T.rex closed around him. All Sam could see were the soles of the Professor's feet as he was lifted up.

"Please. Somebody, help!" came a muffled plea.

Davy looked at his father, who shook his head "no." Davy turned to Rex and nudged him. Rex walked over to his mother and roared.

The mother looked down at her son, turned her head slightly, and then opened her mouth.

A soggy Professor covered with dinosaur spit slid out of her mouth and onto the floor of the cavern.

"Are you all right, Dad?"

"I'm fine, son," smiled Sam.

"I guess we couldn't let Rex's Mom eat Professor Berenson, even if he was going to kill us."

"That's right, Davy," said Sam. "He's got a lot to answer for back home."

"What about Jackson and his men?"

"They seemed to have disappeared."

"The plane. They'll take the plane. We'll be trapped here again," said Davy.

"Once we get back above the valley we can call for another plane," said Sam, holding up the Professor's cell phone.

While Sam Ross held a weapon on a disoriented Professor Berenson, Davy, Margaret, and Gretchen followed Rex and his Mom out of the cavern and back to safety.

Wedges had kept the crevices from sealing again following the explosion, so they were able to climb back up out of the hollow mountain and return to the landing strip on the patch of land overlooking the valley in the clouds.

As Davy predicted, Jackson and his men had apparently escaped in the plane because it was gone. But Sam used the cell phone to contact the Tanzanian government and another plane would be there shortly.

Davy decided to use the time to say goodbye to Rex. Rex, however, had other ideas. He followed them to the air strip and smiled when he heard the sound of an airplane. Rex looked up at the sky and started to nod up and down.

"Rex," said Davy. "You have to stay here."

Rex shook his head "no," and then let out a sobbing squeal.

"Don't cry, Rex."

Sam Ross put his hand on Davy's shoulder.

"He knows you're going away," said Sam. "You have to understand something, Davy. New York is the only home Rex knows. He was born there. He may be connected to this place by instinct, but as far as family goes, you're it."

"Then why can't we take him with us?" Davy asked hopefully.

"Because this is where he belongs. He just has to learn to adjust. Besides, in another year, he's going to be 20 feet tall and a year after that as big as his mother. In time he'll figure it out."

Davy walked over to Rex.

"I wish I didn't have to leave you here, Rex," said Davy. "But that's the way it has to be."

Rex nudged Davy and nodded "no." Rex then nudged Davy away from the rest and pointed with his head toward the valley.

"You want me to stay here?"

Rex nodded "yes."

"I wish I could, pal, but I gotta go home too. I'll come back to visit. I promise."

Rex put his head down and when he raised it back up there was a big dinosaur tear in his eye. Davy felt his own eyes start to water.

"Come on, Rex," said Davy, wiping a tear from his eye. "This isn't easy for me, either."

Rex nodded and then licked Davy's cheek.

Just then a large shadow loomed over Rex and Davy. Davy looked up and saw Rex's mother.

"I'm sure you and your mother have a lot of catching up to do."

Rex looked torn between his mother and his friend. Rex leaned into his mother and then stared into her eyes. Davy wasn't sure, but it seemed the mother and son were communicating on some deep level.

Then the Mother T.rex pushed Rex aside and moved toward Davy, bending down down and reaching out with her right hand. Davy looked at the giant hand of the T.rex.

The mother reached out further and at first, Davy was scared. Then he realized she wanted to give him something. He opened his hand and she placed something in it, then nudged her son, to follow her back into the mountain.

Rex bowed his head, gave Davy another nudge and another lick, and then reluctantly followed his mother. They stopped at the edge of the rain forest, turned, and saw Davy wave at them. Rex waved back at Davy and then stepped into the clouds surrounding the valley just as a cargo plane landed.

"I love you, Rex," shouted Davy, his eyes filled with tears.

Davy watched as Rex and his mother disappeared into the clouds of the valley below. Sam walked back over to Davy and gave his son a hug. Davy couldn't stop the tears from falling.

"I know son," said Sam. "But it's all for the best."

As Sam started toward the plane, Davy looked down at the gift from Rex's mother. He smiled and slipped it into a pocket of his jacket as he climbed aboard behind his father.

They had been airborne for about ten minutes, with Davy and Gretchen sitting behind Sam and Margaret Ross, when Margaret called New York to tell Grandma Becky they were with Davy and were all on their way home. They could all hear Grandma Becky shouting for joy on the other end of the phone.

Suddenly, Gretchen sat up in her seat.

"Hey!" she proclaimed. "What ever happened to the Professor?"

Sam and Margaret gave each other a knowing smile.

In the belly of the plane, amid several boxes and crates, was a metal cage. Inside the cage sat the Professor, looking both forlorn and angry, wondering how he was ever going to get out of this mess.

A Tanzanian guard sat in a chair next to the cage and smiled at the sign that read:

"Homo sapien. Donated by Sam, Margaret, and Davy Ross and Gretchen Tucker."

Back in the passenger section of the plane, Gretchen had fallen asleep next to Davy as Sam and Margaret looked out at a beautiful sunset.

Davy waited awhile longer before he opened his jacket and took out the gift from Rex's mother. He looked down as a small crack appeared in the softball-sized egg he gently held in his hands.

ABOUT THE AUTHOR

FRED YAGER is a business television executive and screenwriter. He was a reporter for the Associated Press for 13 years covering everything from politics and entertainment to general news and crime. He has also worked at CBS News and Fox Television. A member of the Writers Guild of America, several of his screenplays have been optioned. Fred grew up in upstate New York, and now lives in Fairfield County, Connecticut with his wife Jan and their two sons.

Fred Yager is also the co-author of two suspense novels with his wife Jan Yager: *Just Your Everyday People* (Hannacroix Creek Books, Inc., 2001) and *Untimely Death* (Hannacroix Creek Books, Inc., 1998).

Shepherd Junior High
Ottawa, Illinois 61350

Shepherd Middle School
Library
701 E. McKinley Rd.
Ottawa, IL 61350
815-434-7925

Printed in the United States
2309